"You're telling me you bought my computer at an auction?"

"I hope this isn't difficult for you," she said gently.

"Difficult?"

"I don't know…I mean…did Cole survive the war?"

He cleared his throat. "Live and in person."

"So you're…"

"Cole. What made you think I didn't survive? And how did you know I was in the war?"

"I opened your letters."

"You *read* them?"

"Well, I didn't mean to—"

"Reading isn't an involuntary response."

Tess turned to face him directly. "No, but—"

"How much do you want for the computer?"

"Money?"

"Why else would you be here? You know my designs are on the hard drive."

Shocked, Tess stared at him. "I thought if you hadn't survived, your family would want these letters—in case you hadn't sent them. I would've wanted my brother's." Not waiting for his reply, she left his office.

Jerk! She should've kept the damn computer. And here she thought she'd read the letters of the last sensitive man on the planet.

Dear Reader,

Some characters stun us with their capacity for change, some with their amazing ability to hang on to their beliefs despite the costs. I have never been the first one in line for change. It's hard. And sometimes it's scary. But then, it's rare to find something glorious any other way.

This story is about family and how deeply those ties bind us all. Family is very important to me. I have a son serving in the Middle East, whom I worry about constantly, and parents who live across the country, who are an equal worry in a very different way. And I think how lucky I am to have them all.

Please join me in this journey of change, of ups and downs and, of course, of love.

Ever the romantic,

Bonnie K. Winn

RULES OF ENGAGEMENT
Bonnie K. Winn

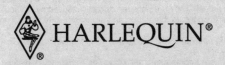

HARLEQUIN®

TORONTO • NEW YORK • LONDON
AMSTERDAM • PARIS • SYDNEY • HAMBURG
STOCKHOLM • ATHENS • TOKYO • MILAN • MADRID
PRAGUE • WARSAW • BUDAPEST • AUCKLAND

ISBN 0-373-71305-3

RULES OF ENGAGEMENT

Copyright © 2005 by Bonnie K. Winn.

This edition published by arrangement with Harlequin Books S.A.

® and TM are trademarks of the publisher. Trademarks indicated with
® are registered in the United States Patent and Trademark Office, the
Canadian Trade Marks Office and in other countries.

www.eHarlequin.com

Printed in U.S.A.

PROLOGUE

RIFLE SHOTS BOOMED across the green-carpeted acres, their echo resounding over the silent crowd. The casings flew harmlessly toward the clouds, yet Tess Spencer felt each volley as though it tore through her heart.

As the twenty-one-gun salute continued, soldiers in crisp uniforms took their mark, shooting in unison, their somber faces reflecting the seriousness of this final honor.

Tess could barely contain herself as she stared at her twin brother's coffin. He was too young, *they* were too young. Even though she'd seen David's face one last time before the coffin was closed, his dark hair and blue eyes so like her own, she wanted to cry out that it was a mistake. David was coming back. He couldn't, wouldn't leave without her.

More tears splashed down her cheeks, wetting the collar of her black dress. Hearing her mother's quiet sobs, Tess looked at her parents' dark heads pressed together. Grief couldn't define their agony. Tears couldn't erase their pain.

Pain that had begun when the chaplain and another officer had rung the doorbell, then explained how David had died on the other side of the world.

An Army Reservist, he had willingly accepted the call to serve. Loyal to both country and family, David hadn't questioned his duty. And he'd assured Tess he'd be home safe and soon. David never broke his promises.

The guns were suddenly silent. Then with great dignity, the soldiers lifted the flag draped over the coffin and folded it into the painfully familiar triangle.

Tess's mother accepted the flag, clutching it close before bowing her head, her body shaking with sobs.

Fingers trembling, Tess reached out toward the coffin. She wasn't ready to say goodbye. *Oh, David. How did this happen?*

Throat raw, eyes burning, Tess felt the start of more hot tears. Her world had tilted and she wasn't sure it would ever be right again.

CHAPTER ONE

Six months later

COLE HARRINGTON gripped the file containing the latest software designs his engineering firm had produced. He'd expected twice as many. Scrapped or missing, he'd been told by his staff. Designs he'd sweated over before his extended deployment to Iraq.

He'd left Mark Cannon in charge of his company, a man he trusted. Or thought he trusted.

Some of his ideas had been good, too good to be scrapped. Had they been stolen? Or worse, secreted out by one of his own people?

Cole looked at his second in command. "I want to know what happened to my work."

Mark scowled, his brown eyes dark with anger. "You think I don't? Fredrickson says some of the designs you're talking about could've been obsolete, that—"

Cole slammed the folder on his burl walnut desk, rattling the mariner's clock on the corner and scattering the morning's mail. "He heads the research and development team, not the company. I *know* my work was good."

"Cole, you've only been back a month. And you've been playing catch-up most of that time. We only found out yesterday the product was gone. How do you know Frederickson's not right? Maybe it was outdated. You were gone a lot longer than you thought you'd be."

"But I didn't expect the company to be run into the ground!"

Mark stiffened. "This isn't the first takeover attempt by Alton Tool."

"It's the first one that might succeed," Dan Nelson, the chief financial officer, warned. "We lost out to them on the last three major bids. We're in deep on research and development with nothing to offset the expense."

Towering over them, Cole looked from one to the other. "We can't let Alton get this bid. It's time to deal with them." Alton Tool had tried everything to get rid of Harrington Engineering, including poaching software designers and the failed takeover. It wasn't a stretch to believe Alton had taken the next step in corporate piracy.

Cole glanced at Nate Rogers, head of security, who wore his military experience like a badge of honor. "I don't want a single paper to get past the exits."

"You got it."

"Any luck finding my laptop, Nate?"

The other man shook his head, his face ruddy beneath white-blond hair.

Cole cursed beneath his breath. The laptop had traveled around the world with him, surviving sandstorms and bullets. And on it he'd saved a copy of his work, including the missing designs. He'd brought it to the office with him when he returned and he wasn't sure just when it disappeared, but he couldn't find it. Dozens of people roamed the halls and he rarely kept his own door locked.

He wished he'd left the computer at his house, even his parents' home. It had been crazy since he'd come back from deployment. Readjusting to civilian life, taking back the reins to his business, finding out the trouble it was in.

"Nate, get a second man looking for the laptop. We find it, we have the designs."

"Right."

There was one notable person missing in the room—Jim Fredrickson. Cole knew the other men had noted the fact, but he wanted to talk to Jim alone.

"Okay, guys, that's it for now."

As they shuffled out, his gaze flicked to each in turn. Nate Rogers. They'd served together in Bosnia. During a skirmish the tall, rangy man had pushed Cole out of the way, taking some incoming shrapnel in his leg. It had busted up his knee, causing a permanent disability, ending Nate's promising Army career. Cole had sought him out when he'd started up his engineering plant, offering him a premium salary to head his security division.

Mark Cannon. They'd worked together for years, developing both a friendship and deep level of trust. Enough that he'd felt secure when the call to serve in Iraq had come.

Dan Nelson was the newest face on his team but also the oldest. He'd worked for the competition. But he was talented, accomplished and had never given Cole a reason to distrust him.

And he was, at most, the numbers man. Not someone who ever touched the creative. Or shouldn't, anyway.

And the missing man, Jim Fredrickson. He and Cole had worked side by side as budding software designers. Logically Jim had the easiest access, but Cole couldn't believe his old friend would betray him. They went back too far. But there were plenty of young designers Cole knew little about in Jim's department, since they tended to come and go frequently. Each one hoped to be the next Bill Gates. Cole had wanted to keep his company small, run it with a hands-on mom-and-pop sense of caring, but the reality of business success was growth. He employed more than two hundred people. He knew a lot of them, but not all.

Cole phoned for Jim to come up. As he waited, he stared out the huge picture window at his plant, which made processing equipment for companies that produced everything from candy to plastics to electronics. His was a hybrid business. One that had to be constantly evolving, thus the importance of the cutting-edge software designs. There was potential for enormous profit. And it enticed corporate raiders like triple-layered, chocolate-decadence cake wooed sugar junkies.

Cole had been protecting his firm since the day he'd opened the doors five years earlier. But its condition had never been this dire. His deployment had lasted nearly a year. And in that time his profitable firm had nearly gone bankrupt.

Bankrupt! Because of the lost bids to Alton Tool. He could still hardly believe it. Although he'd stayed in touch by e-mail, he'd left the firm's management to Mark. He couldn't second-guess it from a combat zone.

He heard a knock. "Jim. Come in. Shut the door."

"Calling me on the carpet, boss?"

Cole took the chair angled next to Jim's. "The missing designs, Jim."

"They aren't missing. I told you. They're old, so they must've been—"

"Scrapped. I know. How well do you know the people in your department?"

Jim shrugged. "I work with them. They're an efficient team."

"No one stands out as overly eager? Anyone working more overtime than you'd expect them to?"

He frowned, thinking. "No one stands out. You remember how it was when we first began. They've got lots of energy and ideas."

Cole nodded. His own surplus energy and creativity had strayed far from the typical, leading him to develop this business. "We're tightening security. That begins with your department. You'll have to keep watch. It'd be easy enough to slip out a CD or a flash point disk loaded with the designs."

Jim scratched his forehead. "Maybe you ought to hire a guard to sit in our department."

"That would boost creativity." Cole ran a hand through his thick, dark hair, already growing out of the military cut. "Good thing I have a copy of the designs on my laptop. Except I can't seem to find that, either. Just do what you can, Jim."

"Sure." His friend stood. "And don't worry so much. This will work itself out. You've got the golden touch."

"Yeah." *Golden.*

THE MAIN AUCTION ROOM buzzed with hushed voices and the rustle of people. The auction had begun, but browsers continued to walk the narrow aisles. Everything from antique sideboards to elk antlers crowded the large room.

Tess and her cousin, Sandy, eyed the new lot the auctioneer was describing, a two-drawer wooden file cabinet and desk. "I need a small file cabinet for home," Tess mused. "But I don't have room for the desk."

"If you get it for a good price, I'll go in with you. The little writing desk Grandma gave me is pretty but I can't fit all my computer stuff on it."

"Okay." Tess was an experienced buyer for furnishings of the Spencer restaurants. The opening bid was low, then two bidders jumped in, vying for the lot. Tess held back until it was down to what seemed to be the last bid. But just as she held up her numbered card, the bidder who'd dropped out reentered the match. Tess lowered her hand.

Sandy immediately jabbed her arm. Hard.

"Fine," Tess muttered, putting her number back in view. "Geez, it's office furniture, not diamonds."

"Sorry," Sandy replied without remorse, tucking her short blond hair behind her ears. "But it's a great desk. I'd have paid that much without the file cabinet."

Accepting Tess's as the final bid, the auctioneer hit the podium with his gavel and she turned her eye to an early nineteenth-century oil painting next on the block that would be perfect in Spencers' Galveston restaurant. Winning the bid at a reasonable price, she leaned over to whisper. "Is that enough for you?"

Sandy grinned. "I'm happy with my haul."

Making their way back to the service counter, Tess appreciated Sandy's upbeat companionship. Sandy and Tess were the same age, thirty, and they'd grown up together, more like sisters than cousins. Tess didn't have any sisters of her own. She and David were the only children in her family. Tess swallowed against the swelling in her throat. Each day since he'd died had been a roller coaster. She could be on a relatively even keel when the smallest thing triggered a rash of memories capable of flattening her.

She couldn't count the times she'd turned to the phone, or walked into his office and for the briefest moment believed her brother would be there. Then the instant remembering, the sudden, fierce pain. Their lives had been so intertwined before his deployment that she'd seen him every day.

As they waited in line, Tess caught Sandy's concerned gaze. "What?"

"How are your parents coping with the restaurant?" Thomas and Judith, Tess's parents, continued to run the original downtown venue, considered the top spot to be seen in Houston.

"They say it keeps them busy. But they're trying to do too much."

Sandy was skeptical. "Unlike you?"

When David's reserve unit had been called up, Tess had taken over the second Houston location David had captained. "I'm just doing my part."

"Overseeing all three locations? You're working yourself to death."

Tess grimaced.

Instinctively Sandy grasped her arm. "I'm sorry. I didn't think before I spoke."

"It's okay."

"Are you ready?" the young cashier asked as the customer in front of them departed.

After paying and arranging to have the desk delivered, Tess picked up the painting. One of the porters loaded the file cabinet on a dolly and walked with them to load it into Tess's Lexus SUV. As the heavy-set man lifted the cabinet into the rear of the wagon, it rattled.

Sandy leaned closer. "I wonder what that is?"

The porter opened the top drawer and reached inside, pulling out a portable computer.

"The owner must have forgotten it was inside," Tess said.

"Doesn't matter," the man replied. "Rules of the auction. It's yours now."

Tess frowned. "That doesn't seem quite right."

He shrugged. "The seller knows the rules when he consigns the lot."

"It *is* a business lot," Sandy pointed out. "It's not as though the computer belonged to some poor widow. The company probably had so much excess stuff they just didn't bother to catalog it."

"Yeah. You're right. And it is pretty beaten up. Okay." Tess put the computer in the front seat and then reached for a blanket to wrap the painting.

"I'll head home," Sandy began. "Unless you…"

"You don't have to babysit."

"That's what family's for, so you don't have to be alone unless you want to be."

Tess hugged her petite cousin, then stepped back. "Thanks. I'm okay."

"You're not, but I won't argue." Sandy hesitated, her blue eyes clouding. "We all miss David, you know."

Seeing Sandy's mouth tremble, Tess reminded herself that they all shared the loss. "I know. It helps."

Tess read the guilt in her cousin's face. Sandy still had her sisters and brother.

She'd never noticed the small size of her family, always surrounded as she was by numerous aunts, uncles and cousins. Not until David was gone. "I'll see you Saturday."

Sandy nodded as she unlocked the door to her sleek Eclipse, parked next to the Lexus.

After their vehicles were started, they honked, an old habit, each making sure the other wasn't stranded by a possible dead battery or mechanical failure.

Tess took the long way home, driving the quiet, curving lanes of Memorial Drive, which divided the huge park of the same name. Even though darkness was falling, she could appreciate the miles of untouched green that wound through the most beautiful portion of Houston's west side.

Calm by the time she reached her town house, Tess parked in the garage. As she opened the car door, the dome light illuminated the laptop. She scooped it up along with her purse.

Molly, her Norwich terrier, barked out a quick, happy welcome. Hector, David's more reserved Scottish terrier, patiently waited his turn as she petted them both. Scotties, known to be one-master dogs, were often standoffish with anyone else. But she'd known Hector since David had brought him home as a puppy, and he willingly accepted her affection. Although he continued to behave as if he expected David to return. Even now he looked at the doorway to see if his master would step in behind her.

"I wish he'd come home, too," she murmured, scratching Hector's upright ears.

He cocked his head, his dark eyes set in an even darker face, fixed on her.

"Better you don't know what I'm saying."

Molly wriggled her smaller red-tan body in between Hector and Tess.

Tess hugged the dog, then set her down. "Don't be jealous. I love you both."

They trotted beside her as she entered the kitchen, dumping her purse and the laptop on the counter. "How about a carrot, guys?"

This was a word they both recognized and loved. Setting Molly down, Tess fished in the vegetable drawer of the fridge for the package of baby carrots. She gave them each one and they peeled out in separate directions to enjoy the treat. Tess uncapped a bottle of ginseng-infused tea, then glanced at the computer.

After flipping open the cover, she plugged in the unit, browsing through the directory. Within a few minutes, she saw that the hard drive hadn't been cleaned by the previous owner.

Designs, Schematics, Financials. Nothing there that interested her. Pausing at a subdirectory entitled "Letters," Tess frowned. *What kind of letters? Dull, boring business ones, no doubt.*

Pulling up a stool, Tess settled at the bar, scrolling through until one file caught her attention. Deceptively simple, it was entitled "Home." Letters home.

Instantly she thought of David, the last words from him.

And she clicked on the file. A letter appeared on the screen, full-blown.

As Tess began to read, she found she couldn't pull herself away.

The days are still full 24/7. I'm so wiped out by night that my cot actually looks good. It'd be like sleeping on a saggy lawn chair if I could feel anything by that point. I come to in the morning and then the day's gone before I can blink. But the weeks and the months, they crawl.

I lost another man today. Specialist Dixon. Michael Dixon. Twenty-two years old, had a girlfriend in Louisiana. He was quiet, but you always knew you could count on him. I wish I'd gotten to know him better, but sometimes that just makes it worse. My unit's feeling the loss. You have to keep on, put it out of your mind, but when it's quiet, you remember. And I think about his parents, the woman he planned to marry. How they'll go on, too.

Tess's breath shortened.

Tell Mom that the First Lady visited the main camp. No fashion updates, though. She was wearing camouflage fatigues. Reporters ate it up. Beats showing what's really going on over here.

It was simply signed "Cole"

Shaken, Tess sat back. This soldier reported a slice of military service unlike anything her brother ever sent. David's letters had been cheerful, mostly full of newsy chatter.

Unexpectedly connected to the author of the letters, Tess opened a second file. This letter was also disturbingly real, expressing the soldier's feelings about the military engagement and the people in the country where he was serving.

Unable to stop, Tess read his anguish for home and family, the liberty he was fighting for, the loss he experienced for the men under his command who'd been killed or wounded.

David had apparently been shielding her from how bad it actually was, which was so much like him. These letters were a window into that world. David's last reality.

And Tess absorbed each detail. This soldier was a person of deep convictions and loyalty. So much so, she was compelled to read the next letter…and the one after that. Time forgotten, Tess continued reading and reacting. And building a link to a stranger who might not have survived the place she now read about.

BY DAWN, Tess's shoulders and back were stiff from crouching over the laptop all night. She forced her eyes, gritty from lack of sleep, to focus until she'd read the final letter. It was as though she'd met Captain Cole Harrington, had spent the night talking with him about his deepest thoughts.

Closing the lid on the computer, she was bereft that there were no more letters. In the space of an evening she knew more about this stranger than she did her closest friends.

And there was the undeniable connection to David.

Her brother had also been a man of ideas and passion. Absurdly, she felt cheated. They had shared everything. David should have shared the final chapter in his life, too. Had he been frightened? Had he experienced any premonition of his own fate?

Tess pushed past the growing lump in her throat as she traced the edges of the computer. She felt terrible about keeping it. The rules of the auction house may have said it was hers, but it belonged to this soldier. The letters were so revealing, she couldn't imagine the owner wishing them to be read.

She bit down on her bottom lip as the worst

possibility pushed to the front of her thoughts. If he hadn't survived, perhaps the laptop had been discarded.

Tess made an instant decision. She would find the owner, or at least his family. They should have his computer.

Tess knew that trying to get any sleep now was pointless. So she brewed some fresh coffee, then took the dogs for their morning walk. After showering and dressing she packed up the laptop and drove to the restaurant. Settled at her desk, she phoned the auction house. According to their records, the lot she'd purchased had come from Harrington Engineering. Harrington. Captain Cole Harrington.

Was he a husband, son…brother?

Tess picked up a phone book. All morning she'd been preoccupied by his fate. Now she felt a personal stake in the outcome.

Harrington Engineering was listed, but she paused as she reached for the phone. This wasn't the sort of thing you talked about over the telephone.

She scribbled down the address. It was midweek, traffic was light and Tess made the trip quickly. Too quickly.

She'd rehearsed what she would say during the drive, but now, parked in a visitor's spot at the front of the parking lot, she still wasn't sure.

CHAPTER TWO

NOW THAT HIS TEAM was searching for the designs, Cole felt marginally better. But they had to show up soon or the bid to Landry Industries would be closed. He'd begun work on the bid when Landry was still debating the new lines, before they'd secured their financing. Now that Landry had gone public, they had deep wells of cash. And Cole wanted some of it to bail out Harrington.

He glanced at the mariner clock. But the hands hung uselessly ever since he'd slammed the desk the day before. He regretted the impulse. His employees had given it to him as a gift to celebrate their first year in business. He wasn't a particularly sentimental man, but he viewed the clock as a good luck token. He'd get it fixed. No sense pissing off the Fates.

He logged on to the network computer. His

e-mail in-box was already full. Hopefully some of it was good news.

Dan stuck his head in Cole's open door. "Do you know where Mark is?"

"Haven't seen him this morning."

The finance officer frowned and, obviously in a hurry, ducked back out and was on his way before Cole could question him.

The bank of phones that connected reception to the line supervisors in the plant were ringing incessantly. Then the outside lines started ringing as well.

"Marcia?" Cole called for the receptionist as he strode down the corridor. Couldn't anyone be bothered to answer the damn phones?

The reception area was empty except for a woman he didn't recognize, and the phone lines buzzed out of control. This wasn't like Marcia. Ignoring the visitor, he walked behind the counter, and took over the switchboard.

"Can I help you?" he asked, once there was a pause in the phone calls.

"Actually, I—"

The phone rang again. "Just a minute."

She pulled a card from her purse and laid it on the counter.

Finally, the board quieted. "Sorry about that. The receptionist is supposed to have been here by now."

As he stood, Marcia rushed in, frazzled-looking. "I'm sorry. My car wouldn't start." She glanced at Tess. "I hope you haven't been waiting long."

"No. Just got here."

"I called the auto club, but it always takes forever. I'm lucky to have such an understanding boss." Marcia glanced at Tess. "Did Mr. Harrington take care of you?"

When she heard his name, Tess stood and addressed him. "Actually, I want to talk to you."

Just what he needed. But the woman had been waiting patiently. He gestured to a chair in the reception area.

"I'd prefer to speak with you in private."

He didn't really have time for this, but he shrugged and quickly escorted her down the long hall into his office. He pointed to a pair of comfortable leather chairs.

"I'm afraid you have the advantage," he began. "I don't know who you are."

"Tess Spencer."

"And you're with…?"

"I work in my family's business. But that's not why I'm here. Well, in a roundabout way it is." She paused. "I'm just making my explanation more confusing." She held up a laptop computer, then placed it on the table that separated them. "I'm here because of this computer."

He barely glanced at it. He didn't need to hear another sales pitch. "Our office manager takes care of all our purchasing needs." He reached for the phone. "I can call her, pass along your—"

"You misunderstand. This laptop... It belongs to Cole Harrington."

He tensed, his amiable smile disappearing. He picked up the computer, recognizing the distinctive gouges. "The one with my schematics," he muttered beneath his breath. "How did you get it? Who are you with? Alton?"

"No. Last night, I went to an auction. I bid on a lot and this computer was in it."

"You're telling me you bought my computer at an auction?"

"I hope this isn't difficult for you," she said gently.

"Difficult?"

"I don't know... I mean...did Cole survive the war?"

He cleared his throat. "Live and in person."

"So you're…"

"Cole. What makes you think I didn't survive? And how did you know I was in the war?"

"I opened your letters."

"You *read* my letters?"

"Well, I didn't mean to—"

"Reading isn't an involuntary response."

Tess turned to face him directly. "No, but—"

"Okay. How much do you want for the computer?"

"Money?"

"Yes. Why else would you be here? You know my designs are on the hard drive."

Shocked, Tess stared at him. "I thought if you hadn't survived, your family would want these letters in case you hadn't gotten to a land line to send them. I would've wanted my brother's. But I'm sorry if reading them was an invasion of your privacy. And I'm sorry you thought I'd sell them to the highest bidder." Not waiting for his reply, she left his office. She marched down the hall and through the reception area.

Back in her Lexus, she ignored the shrill response of her SUV as she put it in gear and sped out of the parking lot.

Jerk! She should have kept the damn computer. And here she thought she'd read the letters of the last sensitive man on the planet.

"MARCIA!" COLE BARKED into the intercom an hour later.

"I'm not deaf," she reminded him.

"Did that woman leave a card?"

"I'm guessing your meeting didn't go well?"

"The card?"

"I'll be right there."

He continued to pore over the computer until Marcia appeared a few minutes later, waving the card at him. "Tess Spencer of the Spencers Restaurants."

The well-known name registered with him as he took the card.

"Was she here to see if we want to participate in one of their fund-raisers? They're always for really good causes."

Cole didn't bother telling her that Tess's intentions were his business. Marcia had cheerfully meddled since her first day at Harrington

Engineering. And because she was wise and kind, not to mention old enough to be his mother, he accepted her small intrusions.

"Not about fund-raisers."

Marcia frowned. "Wasn't there something in the papers about their family a while ago?"

He hadn't been back in the country long enough to catch up on the news, local or national. "Marcia, check with the auction house and see what we've sent over in the past few weeks."

"Sure, boss."

Cole continued combing through the directories of the notebook computer he'd used to write letters to the families of his slain and wounded men.

Even though tactical headquarters housed government-issue computers, he, like a lot of officers, had packed a small PC when he was deployed. Rotations were longer than they used to be and this had sometimes been his only connection to home. And when his unit was able to link up with a land line, he'd let his men use it for e-mail.

The letters all seemed to be there. But the designs were gone. Wiped so clean they weren't recoverable. He knew how to look for their prints. But they'd been thoroughly, professionally erased.

So what did Tess Spencer and Alton Tool have to do with each other?

After a quick knock, Marcia popped inside his office. "Here's a copy of the only manifest this month from the auction house."

Scanning the items, he saw that a notebook computer wasn't listed. Of course not.

Marcia held out another paper.

"What's this?"

"While I was on the Web I looked up the Spencers in the *Chronicle* archives." Her graying eyebrows wriggled with just enough intent to let him know she wouldn't leave the subject alone.

He started to skim the page. But as the content registered, he slowed down, absorbing the details of the article. It reported the death of Tess's brother. Sobered, he read about David's background, his contributions to the community, his close relationship to his family, especially his twin sister.

How had this woman who'd lost a brother in Iraq come to own his computer?

"Tess, is that you, honey?" Her mother's voice reached to the restaurant foyer.

"Yes, Mom. I picked up the mail." She caught up to her mother in the kitchen.

Judith Spencer hugged her, enveloping Tess in the comforting smells of cooking, along with her trademark Chanel cologne. Still attractive at sixty-two, Judith's dark hair was streaked with far more gray than it had been only months before. The lines in her face had also deepened, but it was her eyes that betrayed her pain. Eyes that changed from gray to green or blue depending on what she wore or the colors around her. Tess had inherited her unusual eyes.

And much of her intuition as well.

Judith stroked Tess's long dark hair. "What's wrong?"

Tess shook off her annoyance. "Just more traffic than I expected."

Judith studied her a moment longer, but she didn't press. There'd been so much discussion since David's death they often felt talked out. "It's quiet here this morning."

"Dad?"

"He should be here soon. He's at the linen company, straightening out the order."

"I told you I'd do that," Tess protested. The linen supplier was under new management and they'd fouled up the orders for all three locations.

"He needs to keep busy," Judith explained. "You're back and forth between here and Dav— your restaurant so much I don't know when you sleep."

"At night," she replied with a smile. "Something not only smells good, it smells different. Are you experimenting?"

"I just got some young peas, picked yesterday. I want a sauce that isn't too heavy, but that'll enhance their sweetness."

"You'll create something wonderful, you always do. Although Peter *is* the chef if you run short on time."

"Or energy, you mean. Tess, don't worry about us so much. We're not fragile seniors."

"As though you could ever be considered *senior!*"

Judith laughed. "When you turned twenty-one I couldn't imagine how I'd aged that much. Now, if I could just turn the clock back to then…"

Tess bit her lower lip. If only they could. "I know you're not fragile, Mom. You and Dad have been incredibly strong."

Judith took her hand. "It runs in the family."

Tess felt a rush of appreciation for her parents. They'd been running the landmark Spencers for years now, scarcely slowing down following David's death. In the past she'd always believed they were invincible. "Then let me be strong now."

"I don't think I can stop you. Want to taste the sauce?"

Tess grinned. "Absolutely. Are you going to share the recipe or is it a landmark speciality?"

"I think you can twist my arm. Let me just check on the seafood delivery."

Tess pinched a fresh croissant from a tray on the stainless steel counter, then sat on a stool, dangling her feet as she had when she was a child waiting for one of her parents. She supposed she could get to be eighty and still feel that way in the downtown Spencers. It was the original restaurant in the family business, established by Tess's great-grandparents in 1920.

Back then, being right in the heart of the booming petroleum capital, it had appealed to the newly rich oil barons who claimed it as their own.

By the 1940s it was a hub for celebrities in all fields. The Second World War only enhanced its reputation when the three Spencer brothers went to war and only one, Tess's grandfather, returned. *Heroes,* Tess thought bitterly.

Continuing the legacy, Tess's grandfather had opened two additional locations, one in the prestigious Galleria area and one in nearby Galveston.

Patrons spoke of the original restaurant's unmatched ambiance. Beyond the shimmer of formal china, well-polished silver and flawless linen, Spencers retained its classic Deco style. There was a solidity and elegance to the cherrywood walls and leather seating that only time could produce. Decades.

Tess and David had been groomed in the business since they were able to stand on a stool and reach the kitchen counter. She could remember coming in before opening time as a child, the familiar smells of the restaurant itself—lemon wax, and a mysterious blend of wonderful sauces from the kitchen.

She and David had been taught early on to

respect the furnishings, the employees and the patrons—not necessarily in that order. They'd also been taught to love the business, to depend on its history.

But now she wasn't so sure what to count on. So much had changed…

More than she'd been able to accept.

CHAPTER THREE

COLE TOOK THE TICKET from the parking valet and left his car keys. He studied the restaurant's two-story entrance. This, the second Spencers, was located in the trendy Galleria area that catered to Houston's well-heeled elite. Cole had never cared about being seen in the best spots, but many of the patrons probably did.

Also upscale and elegant, this Spencers had its own unique look. Smart, he thought. The locations didn't compete with one another. It was easy to see why the Spencers were so successful. But their connection to his missing designs baffled him.

"Will you be dining with us tonight, sir?" The attractive hostess was dressed in a white blouse and black skirt.

"I'd like to speak to Tess Spencer."

The hostess didn't allow a flicker of reaction

in her expression. "May I tell her who's calling?"

"Cole Harrington."

"Thank you, sir. Would you care to have a seat while you wait?"

He nodded, then walked down the wide, marble steps that led to the bar. Choosing a table, he barely sat down before a waiter took his drink order. Nearly as quickly, his dark German ale arrived.

"Mr. Harrington?" Tess's voice was polite, but there was a barely detectable edge.

He stood. "Won't you join me?"

She hesitated and Cole sensed it was courtesy alone that made her sit. "What can I do for you?"

"Listen." He made himself smile, knowing anger wouldn't get him the answers he needed. "To my apology, that is. I was rude and I'm sorry."

Her eyes actually seemed to change color as they softened. "I see."

He watched her closely. "It was kind of you to bring the laptop to my office. Most people wouldn't have bothered."

"No problem."

He hadn't seen her make any gesture, however a waiter arrived with a drink for her, then disappeared silently.

Cole lifted his glass. "To people doing the right thing."

"And all they're supposed to believe in," she replied, the light in her eyes fading.

He held his glass midair. "Did I say something wrong?"

"No. It's me, completely. I've been…off for a while now."

"I read about your brother. Is that what you're referring to?"

"Yes."

Her brother had given his life in service. As curious as he was about his missing designs, Cole repeated words he'd had to say far more than he wanted to. "I'm sorry for your loss."

"Me, too." She fiddled with her glass. "Sometimes it still doesn't seem real."

"I know."

"I'm sure you do."

He studied her pale skin. Her grief was the one thing he didn't doubt. "Was David regular Army?"

Tess shook her head. "Reserves. Service is

sort of a family tradition. My grandfather was the only Spencer son to survive World War II. My father served for three years. David wanted to devote his time to the family business, but he wanted to do his duty, too, so he joined the Reserves. How about you?"

"Reserves. I joined because they paid for my education." As he spoke, he saw that she was studying him closely.

"But you stayed."

"For a lot of reasons."

Tess hesitated. "Are you glad you did?"

"Yes."

Her expression shifted. "Oh."

Unexpectedly, Cole felt the same way he did when he was writing home to the families of soldiers he'd lost. "Refocusing your grief into work can help. And it looks like you're doing a good job here."

"Just managing what David had already put in place."

"Then I imagine he'd be proud of you."

Her lips tightened. "He should've had so much more. He was too young to die."

Of course he was. "He gave his life for a noble cause."

"Did he?"

Cole wasn't shocked. Grief had no rules, no set parameters. "Even Solomon couldn't answer that to everyone's satisfaction."

She knotted a linen napkin in a jerky motion. "Maybe. Maybe not. Our dinner rush is about to begin and there's so much I'd like to talk to you about…David, I mean."

He needed to talk to her as well.

"Why don't we meet after dinner?"

Her large eyes cleared marginally. "I usually stop in at the landmark Spencers when I leave…but I could let that go tonight." She pulled a business card from the small pocket of her suit, then scribbled on the back of it. "How about eleven? At my town house? Not as distracting."

"I'll be there."

"Good. Now I'm afraid I have to get back to work."

Cole nodded. "Later then."

He watched her walk away, determined to get the answers she'd hidden under that meticulously polished exterior.

TESS HADN'T ENTERTAINED in her town house for months. Luckily her wine rack was well stocked. And she'd raided the restaurant for some decent nibbles, now arranged on the coffee table. Growing up in a restaurant meant there was always good food on the table whether it was a holiday or watching a game on television.

But the small town house itself wasn't so easily fixed. Between her hours at work and those she'd devoted to Families of the Fallen, her compact home had become a place only to shower and sleep, a repository for clothes and not much else. And it showed. The cleaning service still came once a week so the place was spotless, but it lacked a homey warmth.

Maybe it had been a mistake to invite Cole Harrington here. But she had so many questions. There was so much she wanted to know. And she had no place else to go for answers. David's unit was still deployed and although the officers at the base were polite, they didn't have much time for her.

The doorbell rang and Tess ran nervous hands over the trim lines of her skirt. Belatedly it occurred to her that she should have taken time to change into something casual. The dogs barked frantically as she opened the door.

"Hi." She leaned down, chastising her pets. "Hector! Molly! Enough."

Undeterred, the small dogs pawed Cole's knees, but he didn't look annoyed. He knelt to accommodate their short stature and held out his hands. Sniffing him, they apparently approved as they quit barking.

"Sorry about that," she apologized. "They get carried away with strangers."

"Just being dogs."

He sounded unconcerned and she relaxed considerably. "Thanks for coming."

"I needed the break."

"Were you still working?"

"The work doesn't stop because the clock says it should."

She gestured to the sofa. "Is merlot all right? I know it's not trendy anymore, but my wine choices don't follow fads."

"Sounds good."

He wandered over to her window, glancing around the room as she poured the wine.

She gestured toward the tray of food. "I snagged some food from the restaurant."

He picked up an artichoke puff. "Looks better than the hamburger I had for dinner."

She groaned. "I feel the guilt of four generations. I shouldn't have let you leave the restaurant without insisting on dinner."

"Hamburgers aren't lethal."

Tess sipped her wine. "I'm sorry I read your letters."

"I guess that was because of your brother."

"Yes," she admitted.

She dug a bare toe into the hand-knotted silk rug that covered the oak floor. "I was touched by the way you wrote about the Iraqis."

He shrugged. "They're real."

"And how you wrote about the men under your command."

"Also real."

She swallowed. "Especially the ones you lost." She met his eyes, reacting to their startling shade of blue. She wanted to get past this small talk, to tell him that she felt as if she knew him, really knew him. That she wanted to talk with that man, the one she was sure would understand about David.

"It's all right."

"All right?"

"To ask what you want."

What to ask first? She couldn't decide. So she

talked about David, about who he'd been, what had mattered to him. Then she had to know. "Were you scared?"

"Only a fool thinks he's invincible."

"And you're not foolish." She cleared her throat. "Does it bother you to talk about this?"

"It depends. Some people want to be armchair quarterbacks—telling me how it should have been done. Some people want gruesome details. It's bad enough I lived through that part once. I don't need an instant replay. But you want to know how it was for David. That's different."

"I hate to think about him being scared or alone."

Cole's smile was rueful. "In the Army you're never alone."

"David's letters never told me how it really was over there. It didn't occur to me when I read them that he was still being the older brother."

"I thought you were twins."

"He was born first, never let me forget it." She smiled at the memory. "I wish he hadn't felt the need to be so protective."

"If you're worried that he didn't have anyone

to talk to, don't. That's what battle buddies are for."

"But you wrote letters that went below the surface."

"Most of them were to my dad. He served in Vietnam. I could share things with him I couldn't with other people."

"It's lucky you took the laptop."

He paused for a long time. "Yeah. Lucky." She wondered what he was leaving unsaid.

"Is that something many officers do?"

"Pretty much."

"I keep thinking what a waste it was. All of it. David and the others who died. They had so much to give…now they're just…gone. He never married, didn't have any children. He would've been such a good father." She couldn't hide the entreaty in her voice. "Didn't you feel that when you lost one of your soldiers?"

"I thought a lot of things. Sure, about their families they'd left behind. But, no, I don't consider their heroism a waste."

"When David was deployed, I was a little scared for him, but mostly proud. I believed in what he did, in how important our country and values are, how we have to keep that safe. I could recite the World War II heroics of my grandfather and his brothers by rote. And I'm not discounting what they did at that time. It mattered. *Then* it mattered. It was a different world back then. I don't think there's anything to idealize about this war."

"What do you say to the people who thank us for their freedom?"

"What do they have to say to me? To my family?"

"Every time I lost someone under my command I struggled with what to tell his family, to let them know the sacrifice counted."

"Your letters were kind…insightful," she admitted. "But how do you rationalize the incredible loss of life? Especially young people who haven't really had time to know better? Eighteen, nineteen years old? They aren't even old enough to declare a major in college but they have to decide whether they're giving up their lives? No. It's not right! Not for a manufactured war."

"What we did…what David did…it mattered."

Tess could scarcely see beyond her fury. "When you ask young men and women to lay down their lives, they deserve to know the real reason they're doing it."

"The reality isn't sound bites on the news or the supposedly in-depth reports either. It's seeing the crushing grief, the need for hope and knowing you're it—the *only* hope. And when you lose one of your own people, you mourn the life that could have been. And then you go on soldiering."

Tess wanted to call him an impostor. The man who'd written the letters she'd read couldn't believe it was all right. He just couldn't.

CHAPTER FOUR

COLE WALKED DOWN the long curved driveway, past the patio to the big three-car garage. As he'd known he'd be, his father was surrounded by motorcycle parts and tools. Since Cole's childhood, John Harrington had carried on a passionate love affair with Harley Davidson. Each restoration had led to another. Old and new, he loved them all. With the sole exception of his family, they were his only loves.

As the oldest, Cole had learned his mechanical skills at his father's side helping him restore a 1957 Harley Sportster. Others had followed, but that one had always been Cole's favorite. Since his father had never sold it, Cole suspected he felt the same way.

Cole smiled, seeing that his father was polishing a piece of chrome on his newest machine.

"Here's that industrial solvent you wanted."

"Thanks."

"It's quiet in the house."

His father picked up the can of polish, measuring out a few more drops on to the cloth. "Your mother's either at the donkey rescue or her beach preservation thing."

"Shannon in class?" he asked about his younger sister who attended college.

John glanced at the clock over the work bench. "Uh-huh. But Robbie should be home in an hour or so."

Cole would've liked to see his younger brother but he didn't have the time to wait. "Dad, I need to run something by you."

"Shoot."

Cole laid out what he knew about Tess Spencer, from the missing designs and her return of his computer to the death of her brother in the war.

"I don't know anything about corporate piracy." John put down the chrome tailpipe. "But I can't imagine this woman using her brother's death to get some kind of upper hand over your company. When did you say he died? Seven months ago? And they're twins?" He winced. "She strike you as that cold?"

"I don't know. It just seems awfully suspicious that she brought the computer back wiped clean of all my work."

"Maybe the computer's a coincidence, like she said, something she just ended up with."

"I wonder if someone's playing her," Cole admitted. "To get inside my company. But I can't figure out what advantage there is in letting me know she had the computer."

John shook his head. "Restaurants and technical engineering firms don't seem to go together. Anyone in her family with connections to your line of work?"

"Not that I know of. Yet, anyway."

John picked up the tailpipe again. "Anything I can do?"

"Yeah. Get that bike together so we can go for a ride. I'm going to need a clear head."

His father laughed. "Do my best, son. Do my best."

IT WAS THE CUSTOM of Tess and three of her cousins to meet at least once a month for breakfast. Normally, they saw each other a lot more than that, as well. Or they had, until David's death.

Rachel, Kate and Sandy De Villard, daughters of three of Judith's brothers, had all been born within approximately a year of Tess. And it had been natural to grow as close as sisters. At every holiday and family gathering the four stuck together like a unit. They were fierce guardians of one another's secrets and dreams.

This Saturday they'd decided to meet at Kate's sprawling ranch-style home rather than at the restaurant. Nearly all of the De Villard cousins had worked at Spencers when they were teens. Some liked it better than others. Two of the De Villards, Eric and Joseph, had gone on to get degrees in hospitality and now worked in the restaurant business.

The terrace behind Kate's house led into a lush green lawn and well-tended beds of roses, petunias and daffodils. In the corner, a three-tiered fountain splashed softly against bronze fretwork. The fifty-plus-year-old house sat in the middle of two acres, enough land to ensure privacy, not too much to be unmanageable. Kate had chosen the unpretentious house for its charm and comfort.

Tess stepped through the French doors that led from the living room to the terrace. Like the house, it was so Kate—from the wicker and wrought iron chairs with their plump, colorful cushions to the table Kate had set with fragile china, despite the casual occasion.

"Aren't you afraid we'll break these?" Tess asked as she picked up a dainty cup.

"I'll risk it." Kate, who owned a successful vintage clothing store, hugged Tess, then adjusted one of the freshly cut roses on the table.

"Mimosa?" Rachel asked, entering through the second set of French doors from the kitchen. She carried a frosty pitcher of orange juice and champagne.

Tess hesitated. But she didn't have to be at the restaurant for a few hours. "Sure."

Sandy stood at the outdoor stove housed in a stone alcove along with a grill. "Hey! Perfect timing. Did you get the Shipley's doughnuts?"

Tess pretended to look shocked. "Would I forget?"

Sandy grinned. "My fellow sugar junkie."

Tess had missed these lazy Saturday morning breakfasts. But now there wasn't much time for anything but work. It was a struggle just to find a few hours for the Families of the Fallen.

Sandy joined them, holding a platter with her

signature fresh veggie omelet. "Hope you're hungry."

Tess sniffed appreciatively. "Smells good."

After they were seated at the cozy round table, Sandy served the main dish. She scooped an overly large portion on Tess's plate.

"I didn't say I was starving."

"No, but it looks like you haven't stopped working long enough to eat in a while," Sandy replied. "Who wants Parmesan?"

As Sandy grated the cheese, Tess studied her other two cousins. "This isn't a conspiracy, is it?"

Rachel and Kate appeared innocent, too innocent.

"Of course not," Kate replied.

Rachel started to speak, then sighed. "Yeah. We'd prefer to think of it as more of an intervention, though."

"I haven't joined a cult."

Kate placed her hand over Tess's. "You haven't done *anything,* sweetie, other than work. You're spending every waking hour at the restaurants."

"I don't want to let my parents down," Tess protested. She wasn't ready yet to tell them how much she was volunteering at Families of the Fallen. The controversial group touched a sore spot within her family.

"We know you don't." Sandy fiddled with the serving spoon. "But you're not going to help them by making yourself sick."

"I'm just fine!"

Kate's pretty face was drawn, lined with concern. "You never take a moment for yourself."

"That's not true!"

"When's the last time you had a date?" Rachel challenged.

All three women stared expectantly at Tess. She groped for an answer that wouldn't reveal more than she was ready to tell them. "Thursday."

Matching stares of astonishment gave way to oohs and aahs.

"Who is he?" Rachel demanded.

"Cole Harrington," she replied reluctantly.

"What does he do?" Sandy asked next.

"He owns his own company."

"What does he look like?" This from Kate, always the romantic.

"Nice."

"Nice?" the trio repeated in unison.

"Details," Sandy urged.

Trapped, Tess decided to opt for the truth. "He has these blue eyes, really mesmerizing."

A chorus of sighs greeted this statement, but her cousins continued to stare at her in expectation.

Tess didn't have any trouble remembering his appearance, just putting the image into words that wouldn't intrigue her cousins. "He's good-looking, handsome really. Dark hair."

"Harrington Engineering!" Rachel announced. "I knew I'd heard that name."

Again Tess met three matching stares. "Well, yes."

"About a year ago he made the list of Houston's most eligible bachelors," Rachel mused.

Tess was surprised. "You seem to know a lot about him."

"Financial circles aren't that large," Rachel reminded her. "More like a small town with a very credible grapevine."

"Oh."

Sandy wriggled her eyebrows. "He sounds yummy."

"Yes," Kate agreed.

Years ago, they had sworn never to let a man

come between them. They'd survived a few simultaneous crushes during high school, but they'd never had a serious threat to their pledge.

But Tess didn't want to overplay her nonexistent relationship. "It's not serious."

"Is that why you haven't told us about him?" Kate asked. She looked hurt.

Tess wanted to kick herself. She knew how sensitive Kate was. "Of course not. It's really just begun." She crossed her fingers against the fib she planned to tell. "I saved it to tell you together this morning."

Kate smiled. "Oh! That's wonderful. I'm so glad you've met someone."

Tess tried to ignore the guilt nibbling at her conscience. "It's no big deal."

"No big deal?" Kate looked appalled. "Of course it is. In fact, you have to bring him to the party."

"Party?"

"The anniversary party."

For Kate's parents, of course. "Sorry. I haven't been very good with dates lately."

All three gaped at her. Tess was known for having a mind like a Rolodex, organizing events for family, friends and the restaurants.

Tess smiled. "The anniversary party, of course. I remember."

They didn't believe her. She saw it in their faces.

"You'll bring him?" Kate asked.

Tess wanted to say no, but she had to convince her cousins that she was all right. "I'll ask him."

"Then I'll count on it," Kate replied happily.

"I didn't say he could come!"

"If *you* ask him surely he will," Kate countered.

"Yes," Sandy chimed in.

"My vote's on you," Rachel agreed.

Tess wished it were that easy, that she could simply pick up the phone and invite Cole. He'd be shocked to know he was now the man in her life. Especially after they'd ended the evening on such an antagonistic note. But she didn't see a way to pull her foot out of her mouth.

Sandy lifted her glass. "To Tess and Cole."

Rachel and Kate clinked their glasses with Sandy's, then glanced at Tess expectantly.

Seeing no other choice, she picked up her glass, joining the toast. What in the world was she going to say to Cole?

"So have you decided on the gift for your parents?" Sandy asked Kate. "Or are your brothers still arguing?"

Kate sipped her mimosa. "If it had been up to them, my parents would have gone deep-sea fishing either in Mexico or Alaska, but I held out for the European river cruise to Vienna."

"They'll love that," Sandy agreed. "Even on my budget, I'd have voted for that one."

Rachel reached for a doughnut. "You and Tess sharing these?"

Sandy counted the remaining doughnuts. "Possibly."

"Tess, your mother had the pastry chef design an incredible cake. Did she tell you about it?" Kate asked.

Tess blanked again. "No."

"It'll be fantastic. Be sure and ask her about it. He's going to use their original cake topper."

"That's amazing," Sandy said, wiping her fingers on a napkin.

Rachel groaned. "No wonder you're such a romantic, Kate. It's genetic. You can't escape it."

Tess met Kate's eyes, knowing that in truth her cousin actually guarded her heart. It was one of the few secrets they shared from the others. Kate had been so devastated by a bad experience, she rarely opened herself to new relationships. Tess reached for a gooey, chocolate-filled doughnut, her favorite. So much for romance. Maybe they should buy a cruise for the four of them and just be done with it.

DAN NELSON held the latest financials. "You could accept one of the offers to sell, Cole. It wouldn't have to be from Alton. You'd get out with enough for another start-up."

"I've got employees, including you, who count on their paychecks. After a new owner stripped the place, you'd all be out."

Nelson thrummed his fingers on the printout. "There's another option. Borrow enough to float us."

"I'm running out of property to mortgage. Short of selling a kidney, I don't see any cash looming in the future."

Nelson allowed a few beats of silence. "So, you want me to put together a loan package?"

"Yeah." Cole waited until the door closed to cross to the window. He stared out at the plant. When the building was first erected five years ago, he didn't have a single doubt that his business would succeed. All the economic factors were in place. He'd done his research, put in the long hours. He'd hired the most talented, the most competent people. But he hadn't counted on his deployment.

His fingers itched for a cigarette, but he'd broken the habit while he was overseas. Surviving withdrawal once was enough.

Someone knocked lightly on the door, pushing it open at the same time. Marcia. She was the only employee brazen enough to believe a closed door meant come in.

"Hi, boss. Mail call."

He didn't turn around. "Anything interesting?"

"There's an article in *Texas* magazine about the Spencers restaurants, how they've been in the magazine's top picks every year. Even has something about that pretty Spencer girl."

That did make him turn.

Marcia's smile was wide. "I marked it for you."

Cole picked up the magazine, flipping it to the marked pages. Tess looked almost as pretty in the glossy photo as she did in person. And classy.

He'd noticed that right away. From the sleek cut of her dark hair to the confidence in her walk.

Glancing at the picture of her parents, he saw where she got her beauty. But there wasn't a group picture of them together, he noticed. Maybe the reporter had been sensitive to the painful omission of David.

The article talked about Tess's management style, her stamp on the restaurant scene in general.

Nothing about a boyfriend or fiancé.

And nothing that gave him a clue or connection. He needed a way in. And they didn't have one thing in common that was going to get him there.

CHAPTER FIVE

TESS WAITED until the last possible moment to invite Cole. Her cousins wouldn't be fooled if she invented a reason he couldn't attend.

She expected him to have an excuse for not going to the party with her. To her relief, he accepted. She felt odd asking him, but he didn't sound as though it was unusual.

Because of restaurant events, Tess had an extensive collection of evening wear. But nothing seemed right as she picked through the dresses.

She finally settled on a long-sleeved, high-necked silk that bared her back. Since her hair matched the dark dress, Tess decided to pile it loosely in a topknot. She kept her accessories simple. Diamond stud earrings, heels and a purse just large enough to hold keys and lipstick.

And, of course, a gift for her aunt and uncle.

Since she hadn't elaborated on the reason for the party, she was still trying to decide how to explain it to Cole.

Then there were her cousins. They'd be watching. Like cats on a fence.

She hadn't been on a date since David's death. It was guilt. Going back to her old life didn't seem right. Not when David had no life.

The doorbell rang, and the dogs let out a barrage of barking. Tess glanced in the mirror, then opened the door. Cole, in black tie, was an impressive sight. "Hello."

"Evening. Am I early?"

"No. You're perfect." She bit her tongue. "I mean your timing's perfect."

He bent to greet Hector and Molly, who'd stopped barking as soon as they recognized him.

She checked the clock. "Would you like a glass of red wine?"

"A small one." His glance followed her, taking in the gift-wrapped package on the table.

She poured two glasses, then handed him one. But she didn't raise her glass, nervously running her fingers over the stem. "I should explain about tonight's party."

"It requires an explanation?"

Tess cleared her throat. "It's an anniversary party for my aunt and uncle."

"And?"

"Well, that's it. I just didn't want you to get the wrong idea about the family gathering."

"And what idea would that be?"

Flustered, her cheeks warmed. "My cousins tend to give anyone…new…the third degree."

"I'm not easily intimidated."

She suspected as much, but then she hadn't given him a true picture of her cousin's expectations. "Good."

"Does your family usually have their parties at the restaurant?"

Tess nodded. "At the original location. Uncle Stephen is on my mother's side, but her family took up the Spencer tradition after she married my father. His family is a lot smaller, while Mother's is a mob. Over the years, they've come to blend. We all get along reasonably well, so…" Nerves. She was talking too much. Sipping her wine, she tried to collect herself.

"You're lucky."

"Lucky?"

"Not every family is so close."

"I've always taken that for granted. Dad's

older sisters, Gayle and Ruth, never married. They spoiled David and me—it was great. They did the same for all the kids. At Christmas, it was like having three Santas."

"It sounds almost too good to be true."

"I suppose."

When Cole took the last sip of his wine, Tess smiled. "If you're ready, I'll grab my bag."

He tipped his glass in her direction. "Ready."

Tucked into Cole's ground-hugging Mercedes CLK, it didn't take long to reach Spencers. The valet quickly took their car.

"Good service."

"It's what we're known for."

Inside, Tess led the way to one of the private dining rooms. The room was overflowing with aunts, uncles, their children and significant others. More than sixty people crowded around the bar and buffet tables. She noticed Cole's eyes widen when he saw the overwhelming amount of relatives. "I did warn you there'd be a mob."

"As long as you don't expect me to remember all their names."

She grinned. "On my mother's side there are seven De Villard siblings, three brothers, four sisters. Short version—I have fifteen first cousins and some of them are married and have children."

Her aunt who was being honored that night waved from the head table, but it was impossible to get past the crowd. "That's my aunt Lily," Tess explained, waving back. "It's her anniversary. And Stephen's the one with the rosebud in his lapel."

A waiter deftly swerved by, recognized Tess and paused, offering them champagne.

"I thought you weren't going to stop, Ernie," she teased, picking up a flute.

"These are for the head table," he explained, offering Cole a drink.

"Toasts already?" She smiled. "Then don't let us keep you!"

Ernie was already making his way through the crowd.

"A Spencer tradition?"

"De Villards actually. My hot-blooded French side." She glanced down, not quite meeting his eyes. "Which reminds me. I got carried away the other evening. You were kind enough to talk to me about Iraq and I went off. I'm sorry."

"You're entitled."

"I'm not apologizing for my views, just for blasting you with them. I was brought up to revere the heroes in my family, but I feel betrayed. The president should've done everything possible before going to war. We were misled and that's unforgivable." She paused for breath. "And I'm doing it again."

"Maybe I bring out the activist in you."

"I wouldn't—"

"Tess, who is this handsome young man?" her aunt Gayle cut in, appearing out of nowhere.

"Yes, who?" Ruth chimed in.

Tess made the introductions.

Cole charmed each of her spinster aunts, dancing with them in turn. Tess was charmed as well.

Ruth winked at her, obviously approving of her "young man." And Gayle paused long enough to declare him a young Cary Grant, thoroughly delicious.

Tess couldn't disagree.

Sipping her champagne, Tess felt a bit more mellow. "That was kind."

"They're nice, interesting. But I'd watch out for Gayle. She's a real flirt."

Tess laughed. "That's encouraging news. Maybe she'll meet someone yet."

"Looks like you know enough people to network with half of Houston."

"Not quite. They're retired now, but Gayle and Ruth still have a lot of contacts left from their restaurant days."

"It really is a family operation?"

"Absolutely. My parents run this location. You know about the Galleria. I used to head the one in Galveston."

"You're not thinking about taking the business public?"

She frowned. "No. It's important to my father that the Spencers chain stays in the family. Why?"

"A lot of businesses diversify."

"Not this one." She peered critically at the closest buffet table but could see nothing that needed refilling. The nearest carving stations filled with prime rib, rack of lamb and turkey were also well attended.

"Something wrong?"

She glanced at him sheepishly. "Sorry. Second nature. The banquet captain has everything in hand."

After filling their plates, they selected one of the round tables set for eight.

They were barely seated when Rachel, Kate

and Sandy approached. Tess stiffened. The three would be merciless if they discovered she'd lied about Cole being a boyfriend.

Tess made the introductions.

"Harrington Engineering?" Rachel asked in her pin-a-bug-on-a-microscope-slide voice.

"Yes. Are you familiar with my firm?"

"The name's been bumped around the financial corridor lately."

He frowned.

"Rachel's a financial analyst," Tess leaped in to explain. "And Kate owns a vintage clothing shop. She shows her own designs as well, which are beginning to outsell the other clothing. And Sandy is a teacher."

Cole acknowledged Kate and Sandy. "I'm afraid I don't know much about clothing, but if you designed what you're wearing, then you must be good. As for teachers, I think they should all be paid a hell of a lot more."

"Amen," Sandy replied.

Kate smiled. "Thank you."

"Rachel, are you an independent analyst?"

"No. I'm with Quinton & Holt."

"She's up for partner," Tess told him.

"Really?"

"She's the family financial whiz," Sandy added. "Got a brain that's half computer, half calculator. Damned annoying at times, but she invests enough of my measly salary that I don't have to live like a pauper, so I tolerate her."

Kate jabbed her cousin. "Sandy!"

"She's worried we're making a bad impression," Sandy explained.

Rachel shrugged. "We are who we are."

"Does the anniversary couple claim one of you?" Cole asked.

Kate laughed. "That would be me. Have you met them?"

"Not yet."

"They've been mobbed since we got here," Tess explained.

Kate hooked her arm with Cole's. "Let me borrow Cole long enough to meet Mom and Dad. I promise to return him."

"Amazing," Rachel muttered, as Kate made off with Cole.

"That's our Kate," Sandy said with a touch of envy. "But, Tess, you snagged him. Why have you been holding out? He's gorgeous!"

"Amen," Rachel added, still watching him across the room.

Tess groaned. "We're intelligent, reasonably interesting women. We have more to discuss than men, don't we?"

"Occasionally," Sandy contended. "He seems nice, Tess."

"He is." That she'd learned. And she wanted to learn more.

"I did a little research on Harrington Engineering," Rachel added.

"Rach! You didn't."

"Be glad I did. His firm's in worse shape than I thought. Without a cash infusion, it's going down."

"Is it that bad?"

"Yeah. And the firm's hocked to the hilt. It won't be easy to raise money. It'd be like investing in a burning building."

Sobered, Tess stared across the room. It wasn't right that he should lose his business because he'd served his country. More of the silent casualties the news never broadcast.

Within a few minutes, he headed back with Kate, stopping subtly closer to Tess than the other three.

Marking territory. A primeval instinct or unintentional?

"Would you like to dance?" Cole asked her.

Three pairs of eyes were fixed on her as Tess slipped her hand in his. "Yes."

The band was playing a soft oldie. Tess felt the warmth of his hand on her bare back. As she fitted into his arms, she briefly closed her eyes.

"I haven't told you how lovely you look tonight."

Somehow her knees suddenly weren't quite steady and she wasn't all that sure of her voice. "You look great, too. In your tux, I mean."

"It doesn't get out often enough."

Tess smiled against his shoulder. "I hope it's having a good time."

"I speak for both of us when I say yes."

Now she couldn't possibly confess that she'd called him because of the pressure from her cousins. "I wanted to talk to you again."

"About David?"

She hesitated. "Yes."

There was a commotion at the front of the room. It must be time to open gifts. Lily and Stephen stood at the head table with Kate and her brothers. Tess watched as family and friends crowded around, drinks in hand. She listened as their laughter turned to shouts when the big surprise, the Vienna cruise from their children, was revealed.

"Are you okay?" Cole asked, gripping her elbow.

Tess didn't realize her breathing had grown ragged. "I need some air." They used the short-cut through the kitchen to the street.

She took in a few big gulps of humid air, despite the exhaust fumes from cars speeding past.

Cole waited until her breathing was even. "What was that all about?"

"It gets to me. My family in there celebrating. Life going on as though David's death didn't even make a blip."

Tess felt the warm trickle of tears, but she ignored them. "After David died, I wanted to stop strangers and tell them to remember him, that he mattered! But kids kept going off to school. Women went shopping, men played golf. Every damned freeway in the city was clogged with traffic just like every other day. I know David's not the first person to die. Not the first soldier. And he's not the first person I've ever lost. But David wasn't ready to die! *I* wasn't ready for him to die. My parents weren't ready… And it's not right that the world didn't even pause, not for a second, not one second…." Tess finally ran out of breath.

Skyscrapers towered across the street, blotting out the sky, enclosing the block. Shrouding everything in her line of vision.

"It mattered, Tess. It still does."

Her heart felt heavy, her energy gone. "Some fun evening I invited you to. You've been an awfully good sport. Especially since I have more relatives than God."

He smiled. "Really?"

"That's not even all of them," she admitted, leaning against the cement wall of the restaurant, still shaky from her outburst. "We always have some with scheduling conflicts of one sort or another. We used to get together on Sundays at my grandparents' farm, but we haven't done that since…since David died."

"Can I make an observation?"

"Since I just spilled my guts, I'd say you're entitled."

"Here at the restaurants, you have to keep it all pulled together for the public image. That's got to hurt considering the way you really feel."

"Yeah," she agreed. Funny that it took a stranger to see that.

"Will your family be upset if you don't go back to the party?"

She shook her head. "Not really."

"I bet you know a shortcut to the valet parking."

"I bet you're right."

He didn't drive directly back toward her home, instead taking I-45, which curved around the downtown area. The freeway wrapped around the city, close to the fabulous skyscrapers. All brilliant glass and light, the new buildings stood next to old ones of brick and stone, an incredible architectural competition.

Cole lowered the top on his Mercedes and Tess felt the wind tug at her hair. She didn't care that it came loose and fell down on her shoulders.

They didn't talk for a while as he drove south on the old freeway. It was the route to Galveston, one Tess drove to check on the restaurant there. But she was always rushed, usually in a lot of traffic, never with a handsome man driving her.

She relaxed against the leather seat. In the evening, in the fast car, it didn't take long to get out of downtown. Tess was surprised when Cole drove down the exit to Hobby Airport, Houston's second largest international airport.

"Are we leaving town?"

"I come out this way when I want to untangle my thoughts. Watch the jets take off."

He drove to one of the outlying lots that housed the private hangars and parked near the fence line.

She watched the jets lining up on the runways. Multicolored lights blinked, presumably signaling pathways and queues, mysterious in the darkness.

"Friend of mine works out here." He pointed to a hangar that spelled out Allen Weston's name in neat letters.

"You're an unusual man. I blow up, you accept an invitation to my crazy family party. I let off steam again and you bring me here. If I blow again, do we take one of these jets to Paris?"

"You'd go?"

She held up her purse. "Passports don't fit in these tiny bags." She met his eyes. "Thank you. For getting me out of there. For listening to me."

The darkness shaded his eyes so she couldn't quite read them. "I want to hear what you have to say, Tess. About everything."

"Everything?" She shook her head. "I've said enough for one night. Tell me about you."

"Nothing special."

She tilted her head. "How'd you come to start your own business at such a young age?"

"Just found a segment of the market that's hot, changing all the time. And put together two parts of it so I could make it move faster."

"You're making that sound awfully simple. If it were, other people would have done it. Why you?"

"Because I didn't want to be a software designer all my life."

"What about your family? Do they work in your business?"

He grinned as though the thought amused him. "No. My dad's retired now. And my brother and sister are still in school."

"An old-fashioned family?"

"We're not the Cleavers, no."

A jet began its ascent, engines drowning out any conversation. So she studied him, this man she still didn't know enough about.

CHAPTER SIX

PROTESTERS LINED UP in the streets of downtown Houston, blocking traffic and creating security nightmares for the police. Tess was among them. Her local chapter of Families of the Fallen was one of several groups that had organized the parade.

Military Families Speak Out and the Women's International League for Peace and Freedom wanted their voices heard on a number of issues. And it took parades to get the media's attention. The families were outraged because the current administration had tried to keep the public from seeing dead bodies returned home to the bases, as well as wounded to the hospitals.

Like today's parade, marches at Dover Air Force Base and Walter Reed Hospital had attracted concerned Americans urging an end to the war.

Some of today's banners were angry: Start Telling The Truth! Some were poignant: Mourn The Dead, End The War. The most personal of all were posters of slain sons or daughters in uniform, inscribed with the dates of their short lives.

Months earlier, determined to be part of telling the human cost of the war, Tess had come to view the peace quilt journeying across the nation. Now she had the privilege of helping carry it in the parade.

She also saw veterans in the parade, ones who supported the soldiers, but not the war, just as she did.

A woman stepped forward from the curb. "You should be ashamed of yourself! Our boys are serving over there!"

Tess swallowed. "That's why I'm marching. For them."

"Tell them that!"

"If I keep marching, maybe I'll be able to."

Tess passed the woman and tried to focus on the route ahead, but she was shaking.

An older man walking nearby veered closer. "First heckler?"

"Yes."

"Did good."

"Thanks."

He held up his placard. "It's not pleasant work, but it's worth it."

She glanced at the poster he held, saw the young face on it and nodded. It was heartbreaking, these young lives that had been lost. Casualty counts weren't personal until you looked into the faces, she thought. Which was why getting this message out was so important.

Being the fourth largest city in the country, and George Bush Senior's place of residence, Houston drew a lot of activists and a good audience.

Tess was pleased to see that a lot of media was covering their event. All the networks, and they'd snagged CNN and the BBC as well.

Tess saw a local reporter she recognized headed her way. Although she wanted their message to get out, she didn't want to monopolize the media because of Spencers' high profile. She averted her face, hoping Melinda Mendez would choose someone else to interview.

"Ms. Spencer?" Melinda smiled brightly and held out a microphone.

"Lots of people here to interview."

"You make good news."

Tess knew she couldn't ignore any publicity on her group's behalf. "Good to see you, Ms. Mendez."

"Want to tell our viewers about Families of the Fallen?"

"We're here today to put faces to the numbers people hear on the news every day. Everyone in our group has lost family members in Iraq."

"You lost your brother didn't you? The one who headed the Galleria Spencers?"

Tess readied herself. "Yes. It tore our family apart. But that's the human cost of war. And when you're counting lives lost…imagine all the people's lives they touched, the broken families, the lives that won't be, legacies that have ended. Let's put an end to the counting by putting an end to the war."

"Are you speaking for the Spencer family?"

"I'm speaking for Families of the Fallen."

"Is there anything you'd like to add?"

"Yes. There's another very real cost. Our service people in the Reserves leave careers and businesses behind that are often in ruins by the time they return because of the inordinately long deployments this war demands. We all need to think of what we're expecting of our military."

"Thank you, Ms. Spencer."

"Thank you, Ms. Mendez."

THE AIRPLANE HANGAR was shaded, cool and mostly quiet. An occasional clunk of tools hitting the concrete floor echoed in the cavernous building. An ancient soft drink machine dispensed Coke in glass bottles for a nickel, courtesy of Cole's best friend, Allen Weston. It was one of Allen's many eccentricities. Like the vintage airplanes he resurrected, the nickel Cokes reminded Allen of a time he claimed he should have lived in.

But his friend would be flattened if anything happened to his high-tech big-screen television set. It was one of the dichotomies that made him such an interesting person in Cole's opinion. However, it was baseball that had brought them together when they'd met at the age of six. Trust had sustained their friendship in the ensuing years.

Trust that brought Cole here now. He needed an unbiased opinion. The problem of Tess had rolled around in his mind since the night he'd held her in his arms as they danced.

Cole paused by the Coke machine that stood only as tall as his chest, inserted a nickel and then retrieved the ice-cold bottle. "Why can't the new machines keep the soda this cold?"

"It probably costs two cents more a month in electricity," Allen observed sourly.

"No students this afternoon?" Cole referred to the flying lessons Allen taught that supported his addiction to classic aircraft.

"No. Caught a break when two of my high rollers canceled."

"A break?"

"Yep. I bill them whether they show or not. They can afford it."

Cole grinned. Allen had more entrepreneurial spirit than he admitted. "I went to that party with Tess Spencer."

Allen adjusted a bolt. "And?"

Cole had already told Allen the whole story up to that point. "And I still don't know how she's connected to the missing designs. But I did find out her cousin could be the link."

"Sounds like you've got to find out more about her."

"I don't have enough capital left to hire private detectives."

Allen picked up a shop rag. "I realize I'm an old-fashioned guy, but haven't you heard of dating?"

Cole slowly shook his head. "If, *if* she's telling the truth, she's pretty raw about her brother." There were enough years of friendship between them to leave the rest unsaid.

"You're not seeing anyone right now."

Cole groaned. "I came here to get perspective, not complicate things." He eyed the small bit of soda left in his bottle, then shook it until it started to fizz.

"Not in the hangar!" Allen barked when he saw the bottle aimed in his direction.

Cole grinned as his friend moved away from his precious plane. "Then run!"

Allen didn't stop to see if he was serious, racing out the tall, wide door.

Following, Cole glanced up, catching sight of the small television perched on the edge of Allen's desk. And spread across the screen, Tess on the afternoon news. He turned up the volume. As he listened, his smile faded.

A FEW DAYS LATER, Cole frowned at the fax his bank had sent. The amount they were willing to lend was far less than Cole needed. But the bank was pushing it even giving him this much.

His phone buzzed.

"Boss, Ms. Spencer is here."

He hesitated. "Okay, Marcia. Send her back."

Why had she come to his office? He glanced at the top of his desk. Nothing really proprietary there, but he closed the file he was reading, did the same for the screen on his computer.

His door was open and she knocked lightly. "I hope this isn't a bad time."

He stood. "No. Come in." He gestured to one of the chairs. "Would you like something to drink?"

"Diet Coke if you have it."

He put ice and Diet Coke in a glass, then refilled his coffee mug.

Tess accepted the drink, cradling it in both hands. "Since this is right in the middle of your workday, I'll get to the point."

"Okay."

"At the party you met my cousin, Rachel."

The one who could be using Tess to get inside his company. "Yes."

"I know she probably seemed brash." Tess

paused. "That's Rachel. Thing is. She's done some checking on your business."

Cole tried not to react.

Tess leaned forward. "Look. I don't know a delicate way to put this. I know you're in financial trouble."

He struggled to stay calm. "That's overstating the situation."

"Well…you know I'm having difficulty reconciling David's death…believing it mattered. And it's not right for you to lose your business because you went to Iraq either."

"Mine wouldn't be the worse loss."

Her eyes remained troubled. "Thank you…. Anyway…the money's why I'm here. David named me as beneficiary on his life insurance. It's a sizeable policy. I haven't been able to decide the best way to spend it."

"There are veterans' organizations that need donations. The hospital auxiliary could really use it."

"I want to loan some of it to you, or invest it in your company, whatever's best."

It took him a moment to comprehend what she was saying. "Me?"

"Yes. It would be as though David was helping someone who'd gone through the same experience. And you told me you hire a lot of vets."

"You can't loan me money!"

"Why not?"

"Because…because you can't."

"That's not a very good reason," she said, an innocent logic to her tone that he didn't dare take at face value.

Her large blue-gray eyes held his. "Tess, you barely know me."

"Is that what you'd tell another investor?"

"David left the money to make sure you'll always be protected."

"My trust fund will do that. My grandparents set it up for David and me. Unfortunately, now I don't have to share it. The Spencers restaurants have been doing well for generations. If they failed and closed tomorrow I still wouldn't have any financial worries. I *am* well protected."

"Tess, a small investment won't help," he replied, not about to allow her a financial hold on his company.

"I'm not talking about a small investment." She pulled a check from her purse.

It took him a moment to register the number of zeros.

"Please accept it, Cole. Call it a loan or an investment, whichever you prefer. I know David would be happy to know he's helping."

It was a brilliant strategy. She could call the loan and he'd be sunk. As an investor, even if she didn't take over, she'd be able to vote her stock. "Tess—"

"Forget that I'm a woman."

He stalled. "Have you discussed this with your parents?"

"It's my decision. Cole, I can't stand the thought of you losing everything you worked so hard to build. David would've been devastated if he'd come home to find the restaurants in trouble." She leaned forward again. "David's life wasn't just the business, but it was important to him. Like your business is to you."

"It's kind of you to be concerned, but you can tell Rachel her radar's off this time."

"Really?"

"Really."

Tess smiled, looking relieved. "That's wonderful! But if that changes, the offer's open."

"Do you worry this much about all returned soldiers?"

"Only the ones I get to know through their letters."

His gut tightened at the reminder. She was still his only link to those designs. "Can you ride?"

She looked intrigued. "A horse? Yes."

"Are you busy tomorrow morning?"

"I think I can get away."

"Good. I'll call you tonight with the details."

He watched until she was out of sight. Despite intuition, and the caution he'd learned as a soldier, she was harder to read than all the insurgents he'd faced.

"TWO DATES in the same week?" Sandy drawled as they walked into Tess's favorite shop. "Am I dreaming?" She thumped her head. "That's right. They're *your* dates."

"I'm sorry it didn't work out with Greg."

Sandy paused at a rack of casual blouses. She picked a shirt from the rack, scrutinized it, then put it back. "Why? It wasn't going anywhere. I suppose I should have pursued it more. As Rachel pointed out when she set us up, he has a *six-*

figure income. Point being, I need to find a guy with money since I don't have any of my own."

"She just worries about you. But I did think Greg was more her type that yours."

"She needs someone who can slow down long enough to take care of her once in a while. Not that she'd ever admit it. And that wasn't Greg."

They wandered through the aisles. Sandy paused at a display.

Tess spotted the wispy, totally impractical dress at the same time as her cousin. "It's perfect for you."

"And not in my budget."

"It's my treat."

"Nope."

"Why not?"

"It's not right."

"Right? You teach because of the children. You're on committees to help get the salaries you deserve. You work extra jobs. Short of giving up sleep, what can you do?"

Sandy frowned. "You shouldn't have to be bailing me out."

"I'm not bailing you out, I'm just treating today. If I'd chosen to teach, I'd like to think you'd be doing the same for me."

"Of course," Sandy agreed.

"Then?"

"Fine, Auntie Tess. I'll try it on."

"The hat, too."

"Sheesh, you're pushy."

While Sandy found the dress in her size, Tess collected the shirt her cousin had been eyeing and put it in the dressing room as well. She'd wait for the right moment to finally tell Sandy that she'd put some of David's money in a trust fund for her.

"Aren't you supposed to be finding a new outfit for riding?"

"Jeans and a shirt," Tess agreed. But boots, like old friends, were better well worn and broken in, so she wasn't shopping for new ones.

"Then let's find your outfit instead of stuffing my dressing room."

"You know, the lottery people make it seem easy, giving money away."

"We're going to have to go to the western store for the jeans, you know…" Sandy looked up from the blouse. "What are you talking about?"

"When Rachel told us Cole's business was in trouble I tried to loan him some money."

Sandy's face sobered. "You didn't."

"Why?"

"It's not like buying an outfit for me, Tess. Putting money into a relationship changes people. I'm guessing this was serious money."

Tess nodded.

"You lead with your heart, Tessie. And men don't understand that's pure."

"It was David's insurance money. I thought I could use part of it to help him."

"That's so, so *you!*"

"Well, just like you, he said no."

Sandy hesitated. "Maybe that's for the best, sweetie."

Tess didn't like the expression on her face. "What is it?"

"Nothing."

"What?"

"You're sure he won't think you're trying to…well, buy him?"

Horrified, Tess stared at her cousin. "It never occurred to me."

"I shouldn't have said anything."

"Even though it was to bail out his business?"

"Maybe he's the exception. Besides, it's done now. You can't take it back."

CHAPTER SEVEN

THE STABLE was located right in Houston, on one of the city's unique plots of unfettered land. Despite the miles of concrete that led in every direction, the grounds comprised acres of verdant grassland. The humidity and frequent rain caused Houston's vegetation to grow as lush as a tropical rain forest. The grass, a matchless emerald-green, had recently been cut, lending its pungent aroma to the clean air.

Cole had ridden at this stable since he was a boy. While he loved riding in the countryside that fringed the city, it was rare to find enough time for the journey. That had been true when he was a child, too. The already overcrowded city continued to grow, spreading out, taking over the small towns at its borders.

Spotting Tess's Lexus, he waved and crossed the yard.

She climbed out of the SUV. "Isn't it a delicious day?"

"Good one for riding." He gripped her elbow, guiding her to the hitching post. "I've had two horses saddled up, mine and one of the stable's."

"I didn't know you kept a horse here."

"For convenience. I have a ranch but I can't get out to it very often."

"You must miss it."

"All my time these days goes into the business."

Her expression faltered a fraction. "Yes, I can imagine."

Tess stroked the muzzle of the horse that belonged to the stable.

"That's Sugar," he told her.

"The rental."

He was surprised she'd known which was which.

"What gave her away?"

"Her age, temperament. Not to mention yours is a stallion. What's his name?"

"Snickers," Cole said.

"I bet there's a story behind that."

"Yeah."

"You'll have to tell me while we're riding. I

don't imagine Sugar gets up to a gallop very often." Tess untied the reins and in one smooth motion mounted up.

Snickers hadn't been ridden for a while and needed a firm hand not to leave Tess and Sugar behind as they rode in the secluded area.

Trees flanked the open space, blotting out the sights and sounds of the city. Tess sat her horse with the ease of experience.

"You must have had years of lessons."

"My grandfather had all of us on horses out at his farm practically by the time we could walk." She chuckled. "I've mucked out more stalls than I'd like to remember."

"When I was a kid I used to wish we had our own place with horses."

"Is that why you bought your ranch?"

"Yeah. For all the good it does."

"You're spending all your time at work now that you're back?"

"Pretty much."

"Me, too."

"Really?"

"Afraid so. My dad's always wanted Spencers to run the restaurants so I'm covering two instead of one."

"How are your parents doing?"

She hesitated. "I'm worried about my dad… actually both of them."

He slowed Snickers to a walk.

He doubted she could fake the pain that surfaced in her eyes. "They're trying too hard to keep working as though nothing happened."

"Maybe your parents would rather be busy."

"Distractions are good, but I don't want them to be stressed about the restaurants."

"Dicey."

"They think they have to be strong for me."

"Tess, they're your parents. That's not going to stop."

"I suppose."

Sugar, her old horse, ambled along. And Cole had no trouble keeping his horse under control. Tess was impressed. Not that she had any latent cowboy fantasies, but she'd always admired the strength and skill it took to control a spirited horse. They were a good match, this bold man and his horse.

"So, Snickers. Unusual name."

He laughed. "When he was a colt, I'd come to the stables whenever I could squeeze in the time. That usually meant around lunch, which

I didn't have time to eat, so I'd grab a candy bar and put it in the same pocket with his carrots. He'd sniff my shirt and try to reach for his treat. The first time, he wound up with my candy bar before I could stop him."

Leaning forward, Cole patted the stallion's sleek neck.

"I'm sorry," she blurted out, unable to keep it in any longer.

"About?"

"Yesterday." She gazed at the alley of trees that stretched out on either side of them.

"Let's stop for a while." Reining their horses in, the two dismounted.

Cole tied their reins to a nearby oak.

"I'm sorry," she repeated, "about giving you the wrong impression."

He stilled instantly. "What do you mean?"

"When I offered you the loan. I didn't mean to offend you."

"I don't remember saying I was offended."

Tess fit her hands into the pockets of her new jeans. "My cousin, Sandy, you—"

"Met her, yes."

"She pointed out that it might've seemed in-sensitive."

Tess wondered at the change in his expression.

"Uninformed."

"I'm glad your business isn't in trouble, and like I said, the offer stands if you do need it. But I have good places to put David's money. I gave a check to Families of the Fallen."

He frowned.

"I'm part of the local group. And I see the effects of the losses right up close. I was part of the demonstration yesterday."

"Yeah. I saw you on TV. Do you think that's fair to the troops still over there?"

"How can you say that? *You* had to write some of those letters…." Remembering the letters he'd written, the one her parents had received, clogged her heart. "Aren't you mad as hell that they never found any weapons of mass destruction?"

"Aren't you proud of what we've done?"

She had been, at one time. "What good has the war done?"

"I'm not a politician, Tess."

"Neither am I."

"You aren't the only one who saw the effects up close, you know."

She started to shake.

Without thinking he put his arms around her. "I know what you've lost, Tess." He smoothed her hair, feeling her pain. Despite his suspicion of her, he knew that was real. Gut-wrenchingly real.

THE ROUND TABLE in the conference room was piled high with financial reports. The halls were full of employees rushing to their offices after quick breaks. No one was taking a full lunch. The situation was too desperate. Every loan Harrington had applied for had been turned down. Everything rested on this final loan package they were putting together.

"Dan, status on the new loan proposal?" Cole asked.

"The accounting department will be working all night. I'll have it together by tomorrow."

Cole turned to his security chief.

Nate shook his head. "No leads on the stolen designs. And the security reports don't show a damned thing out of the ordinary."

"Jim, how are the new designs coming?"

"Right on target. And they're good. If you can keep us hobbling along, we'll get the Mason bid."

"I'm counting on it. Otherwise…"

Without the loan they wouldn't even get the chance to find out if they could've had a chance.

PALM TREES and exotic bamboo reached the third-story glass ceiling in the atrium of the midtown bank Cole had been dealing with since college.

His bank officer sat behind a solid, unyielding cherry desk at odds with the free-spirited architecture. "I'm sorry, Cole, but my hands are tied. You're stretched so thin the bank can't recover a sufficient debt ratio now. Have you considered taking on an investment partner? Or merging? Alton's been interested."

"You aren't by any chance Alton's banker, too?"

"No. But the financial corridor's buzzing. Alton wants to expand. You've got talent and the setup they wish they'd thought of. They've got cash. It's a natural."

Not to Cole it wasn't. "Not interested."

"What are you going to do?"

"Don't count me out yet."

"Glad to hear it."

"Oh?"

"Proud of your service in Iraq, Cole. Damned shame if you lost your business because of it."

"Yeah."

"But don't forget you still have options."

Yeah. Options.

HIS PARENTS' HOME was all noise and confusion when Cole opened the back door.

"I *can't* use Robbie's car," Shannon complained.

"It's only for two days," his mother replied. Then catching sight of Cole, she let out a whoop. "About time. I was going to send out the troops!" She hugged him. "I miss those hugs when you're on the other side of the planet."

His siblings launched themselves at him as well.

"Hey, munchkins," Cole protested.

"Tell Mom I can't be seen in Robbie's *disgrace* of a car at college," Shannon complained after disentangling herself from Cole's hug.

"Tell the princess I *need* my car," Robbie shot back.

"Shannon, I'm not going to rent a car to preserve your image," their mother replied. "And, Robbie, it's two blocks to school. If you somehow can't manage to walk that distance, I'm sure one of your friends will give you a ride."

"Mom!" Their mother ignored their mixed chorus.

"Cole, have you eaten dinner? I made your favorite red sauce enchiladas, and I have a cake."

His father, always the quietest one in their family, uncapped a beer and passed it to him, joining him at the table. "I think I can eat another enchilada, too."

Like pulling on his favorite sweater, nothing fit quite like home. Cole hadn't thought he could eat, but found he was famished. "I used to dream about these." He'd eaten two of the large beef enchiladas. As he reached for a third, he saw his mother wipe away a tear. "Hey, you're not supposed to cry *now*."

"I know." Claire squeezed his arm. "It's easier when you're here because I don't have to deal with my imagination." She let his arm go. "Your food's going to get cold. I have some of that mango salsa you like, too. Mrs. Early canned a batch when she heard you were coming back."

"It's okay, Mom. I don't have to eat everything the first few months I'm home."

"I keep telling myself that." But she rummaged in the pantry anyway.

"She's convinced they're going to deploy you again tomorrow," his father confided.

Cole sighed. "That's unlikely."

"But not impossible?"

"Highly unlikely, Dad."

"Then what's wrong?"

"What?"

"You've got that same itchy look you had when you wrecked my classic GTO when you were in high school."

"Yeah?"

John nodded.

No sense stalling. "I might lose the business."

Claire stopped her search and rejoined them. "Oh, Cole."

"There has to be something we can do," John said. His parents looked at each other. "We'll mortgage the house."

"No."

"And we have savings."

"I'm not taking your money."

His mother's Irish temper flared. "Why not?"

"At this point, it would just go down with the business. You want that to happen to Shannon and Robbie's college money?"

"We want to help you," his mother insisted, not ready to relent. She had a wide stubborn streak.

"I know."

"If you hadn't been deployed for so long this wouldn't have happened," she said into the quiet.

Maybe not, but he didn't want to argue that point with his mother.

"And that's not what you want to hear," she said less than a moment later. "Don't reject our offer out of hand. Shannon's in her last year of school; Robbie's got a good shot at a soccer scholarship. Your dad and I don't need this big house."

"I'll think about it, Mom."

"And now you'll want to talk to your dad, so I'll sort out your brother and sister."

Cole and his father sipped their beer in companionable silence for a while.

Finally John set his bottle on the table. "You won't take the money."

"No."

"What are you going to do?"

"I'm not sure."

"Is there anything else?"

Cole stretched, then told him about Tess's offer.

"What's your gut instinct?"

"Mixed. She *must* have an agenda, big, blue eyes or not."

"Is there a chance she doesn't know the computer's stolen?"

"I don't see how." Cole explained Rachel's relationship.

"But there's her brother."

"And that's another thing. She's involved up to her neck with Families of the Fallen."

"Son, people react differently to service. Soldiers go to war with expectations…"

Cole nodded. His father's war had a thirty-year cloud hanging over it that had never cleared.

"So…" John began again, "if you don't take her loan or ours, then Alton or some other outfit takes over, strips down the business, gets rid of your employees?"

"Yeah."

"I don't see where you have much of a

choice. At least with a loan, you've got a chance."

"I suppose."

"Those vets you hired with mental health issues aren't going to last long under someone new."

Cole had been thinking about them, along with all his other employees. Their jobs would all be in jeopardy. His guess would be less than twenty percent would survive a takeover. His executive crew would be terminated, along with management. And if Alton was the one who got the firm, he might keep the essential personnel just long enough to learn how to run the plant, then let them go.

John pulled two more beers out of the refrigerator. "I can raise quite a bit with the bikes. They're worth a lot more now than fifteen years ago when you went to college."

It took him a minute to answer around the lump in his throat. "And sell my birthright? I don't think so. I have about a week. If nothing else turns up, I'll talk to Tess."

THE DAYS SPED BY as though in a foot race with the calendar. Cole rubbed his forehead, trying to erase the headache that had plagued him for hours. The glare of the computer screen was imprinted on his retinas. He'd studied report after report, but he wasn't seeing any answers. And he wasn't any closer to knowing why his firm had fallen so hard and so fast.

At the quick, rhythmic rapping on the door, he was pleased to see Allen standing there.

"Hey, come in." Cole stepped around his desk. "What pried you away from the airport?"

"The fact that it's after ten o'clock had something to do with it."

Cole hadn't even noticed that it was dark. "I wasn't paying attention."

"The cleaning crew let me in."

Allen must have used the security badge Cole had given him when the company first opened.

"And they were about to leave," Allen added. "As fascinating as this looks, can I drag you away for some dinner?"

At the mention of food, Cole's stomach grumbled. It had been a long time since he'd grabbed a bagel for breakfast. Lunch had been lost in a vacuum of work. "Might as well. I'm not getting anything accomplished here."

Both by habit and mutual agreement they

headed to their favorite steak house. The beer was cold, the steak tender and the baked potatoes were loaded to the hilt with vein-clogging condiments. Two widescreen TVs played nonstop sports. It was a great place to zone.

A bowl of warm roasted peanuts, still in their shells, arrived with the beer.

Cole shucked a few, realizing how hungry he was. "I think my brain's fried."

"Nothing's turned around?"

Cole shook his head. "It's sinking while I watch."

Allen winced in sympathy. "I've got some savings set aside."

"Good. If I lose everything, I'll remember that."

"I guess it's not enough to help."

Cole cracked open another peanut. "If I could figure out what happened to the designs… If I could *find* those designs…"

"What about Tess Spencer?"

"I took your advice."

Allen didn't hide his interest. "And?"

"We've gone out."

"And…?"

Cole shrugged. "What do you want me to say?"

"Is she a spoiled rich kid?"

"When we went riding she was a natural. Showed up with her hair in a ponytail and boots as old as some of your planes."

Allen added a touch of salt to his beer. "Maybe she's just a nice woman whose family has a lot of money."

"Did your mother read you too many fairy tales when you were a kid?"

Laughing, Allen put down his beer. "She really has gotten under your skin."

"What's that supposed to mean?"

"Just what I said."

Cole shook his head. "Nah."

"So what's the problem?"

"I'm not psychic. I can't figure her out."

"Maybe you should have taken her money." Cole snorted.

"What about the bank?"

"Tapped out. I've mortgaged everything except my kidneys. There's nothing left."

Allen plucked a peanut from the bowl. "You sure you don't want to take her money?"

"I'd be the worst kind of fool, giving her the right to call the loan."

"It could be okay."

"Yeah." Cole hated that saving all he'd worked for came down to this.

The waitress arrived with large, full plates, exchanging their peanuts for hot dinner rolls. The "black and blue" steak looked perfect, charred on the outside, rare on the inside. And the potato was gorged with sour cream, butter, chives and cheese. But his appetite had dried up. Allen was right. He was flat out of choices.

CHAPTER EIGHT

THE BRIGHT SUNNY MORNING was too cheerful for Cole's liking. He wanted gloom, some of Houston's predictable monsoon rain, maybe a little hail. At least a few dark clouds.

He'd stopped by Tess's office at the restaurant, but was told she was working at home that morning. Standing at her door, he rang the bell. The dogs barked immediately, then he could hear them pawing at the door. But it took so long for the door to open, he began to wonder if Tess was really home.

Dressed in a thick chenille robe, her hair pulled back in a ponytail, her nose bright red, she clutched a tissue in one hand as she tried to keep the dogs back with the other. "Hello." But it came out sounding more like "hebbo."

"I'm sorry. Your staff didn't tell me you were sick."

"Dey don't know," she said, ending on a sneeze.

"Are they deaf and blind?"

She sneezed again as she invited him in. "'Scuse me?"

"Do you have orange juice?"

"Juice?"

"Or soup?"

She sighed, then waved toward one of the kitchen stools. "I have coffee." It came out sounding like toffee.

"You run a restaurant and you don't even have soup?"

She looked horrified. "You won't tell them I'm sick?"

"Sit down. We may be able to come to an understanding." He twitched uncomfortably between his shoulders, then remembered how many people were counting on him. "I've come to reopen the discussion on your investment in my firm."

She nodded.

"While we're talking I can stock your kitchen."

"O'tay."

"And work out what to tell your family."

She sneezed.

Which seemed to say she agreed.

He phoned his mother and asked her to cook her chicken soup that he knew from experience cured the worst cold and flu symptoms. Then he phoned Marcia and asked her to shop for all the flu-type necessities and bring them over right away.

He opened the refrigerator, found lemons, squeezed them into water he heated in the microwave and added honey. "I'm guessing that bar stool's not the most comfortable chair in the house."

She shook her head.

"The living room?"

She headed that way, settling into one of the overstuffed chairs.

He handed her the hot lemonade.

"Thanks."

She looked so miserable he hated to talk business, but he didn't have any days left to delay. "When you offered the investment from David's insurance, I was anticipating a bank loan."

Crinkling her nose, she lifted the mug. "Now?"

"Now I could use your help."

"O'tay."

Okay? Just like that? "And your conditions?"

She swallowed some of the lemonade. "Dis is good."

"I'm glad. Um, did you hear me?"

"About?"

"I asked what your conditions would be on the loan?"

"No…" she swallowed again "…conditions." She leaned her head back against the cushion.

Whatever he'd expected it wasn't this.

Then she lifted her head. "Check."

"Drink your lemonade."

She curled her fingers around the mug, her shoulders shaking as though cold. "Okay."

Even without makeup, her nose red as fire, she looked pretty in a princess sort of way, all scrunched up in that ridiculously oversized robe. It didn't make any sense. He'd never been drawn to women with money. Who ever said no to them? And when this one was dressed in de-signer suits she looked rich and untouchable. But all curled up with her toes peeping out of flannel pajamas she looked so vulnerable. And that didn't compute.

He shifted nervously.

"Check," she said again, putting her mug down on the side table. And when she got up he didn't stop her.

Vulnerable? She was probably going to head for her study to draw up an ironclad contract for him to hand over his company in exchange for that check.

While she did, he wandered into her kitchen and used her fancy coffee machine to brew some fresh coffee with imported coffee beans. He searched the cabinets and found some English shortbread. The buttery cookies made a decent breakfast. The phone rang once, but the machine clicked on after a few rings, taking the call.

After more than half an hour, he started to pour a second cup of coffee when a thought hit him. Her town house was small and he hadn't heard any noise from her direction. Even the dogs were silent. "Tess? You okay?"

No answer.

Abandoning the coffee, he entered her study. She sat at her desk, her head on her arms. Gently he shook her shoulder. "Tess?"

She blinked, then focused. "Hebbo."

"Hello, yourself."

"Check."

He smiled. "So you keep saying."

She blinked again, then rubbed her eyes. "It's in here." She opened the middle desk drawer, pulled out a portfolio checkbook and reached inside. The check she'd offered him before, already filled out, was tucked inside. She handed it to him.

He hesitated for only a moment before accepting it. "Thank you."

She sniffled. "Welcome."

"You'd better get to bed."

"But—"

He ushered her from the study to her bedroom, pulling back the covers on the bed. "Climb in."

"But—"

"You have to figure out a long-term plan for the restaurants, Tess, even though your dad wants Spencers to run them. You can't do it alone, Wonder Woman."

Then he took pity on her. Not because she was weak. Because she kept on fighting, flu, watery eyes, shivery limbs and all. "But you don't have to figure it out today. Get some sleep. I've got reinforcements on the way, that orange juice I promised."

"But—"

"Sleep. Even fighters have to rest."

Her eyelids wavered as he pulled the plump comforter up over her arms, tucking it under her chin. Her eyes opened one more time. "Thank you."

He really wasn't sure what to make of this woman.

BY THE TIME Marcia arrived with the groceries, he'd pulled himself together. Sick people had always brought out his sympathetic side.

He gave Marcia the check to get back to Dan as quickly as possible. The sooner it was deposited, the sooner the buzzards would stop circling.

Tess continued sleeping, her small dogs planted in her bedroom, both looking sad. He'd put food and fresh water down for them in the kitchen, but neither had been interested.

He used his cell phone to conference Mark and Dan, whom he'd met with late the night before, coming up with a backup plan in case Tess didn't agree to the loan. And now that she had, the other two men were frantic—elated they'd been saved from shutdown and stunned there were no formal loan papers.

"What if she calls the loan tomorrow?" Dan asked on speakerphone from the office.

"She's too sick to demand much more than orange juice right now."

"Without signed papers, she'd have to go to court," Mark pointed out.

"Let's enjoy being solvent for at least twenty-four hours before we panic," Cole suggested.

"When will you be back at the office?"

"Soon." He didn't want to explain by speakerphone that he was waiting for his mother to bring soup. He checked his watch. "Let's plan a meeting at two with Jim and Nate."

He made some more calls, then heard a quiet knocking at the door.

"Hi there," his mother greeted him, holding a tureen of soup, a canvas bag looped over her arm.

He took the soup and kissed her cheek. "Thanks, Mom."

"I didn't even know you'd met someone," she said quietly. "Much less that you're to the nourishing stage."

"Big assumption, Mom." He put the bowl on the counter, inhaling the familiar smell of her unmatched soup.

"I think it's sweet."

"She's more of an associate."

"That you wanted emergency chicken soup for?"

"It's a long story, Mom. But it's saving my business."

Her expression cleared and her canvas tote rattled to the floor. "Cole!"

"Yeah."

She almost laughed out loud, remembered the sick girl, then did a silent cheer and whirled him around in the kitchen. "I have to meet her."

"Good. I was hoping you'd look in on her. She's in bed. I feel kind of awkward."

She smiled again, her motherly smile. "Sure."

The dogs rose to inspect Claire in the bedroom. They sniffed thoroughly, but seemed to decide she wasn't a threat. Then Cole took them to the kitchen.

Claire adjusted the shutters, trying to be quiet, but the noise woke Tess. "I'm sorry, Tess. I didn't mean to wake you. I'm Claire. Cole's mother."

"Hebbo."

Claire smiled. "I see I'm not any too soon with that soup. How are you feeling?"

"O'tay."

"Do you feel like sitting up?"

Tess nodded.

Claire adjusted her pillows, fluffing them into a comfortable position and straightening the comforter. "I'll just be a minute."

Still woozy, Tess watched the attractive woman disappear, then glanced down, looking for the dogs. They weren't anywhere in sight. It was like waking up in the middle of a movie. She was in her own bed. Her dogs had disappeared. But a stranger was offering to bring her food. And her tongue felt as if it had swollen to about four times its size. Maybe it was an alien kidnapping movie.

Claire returned with a tray. Tess recognized the tray as hers. The dinnerware, too.

"This was always Cole's favorite soup when he was sick. Actually all my children's. He has a younger brother and sister, you know." It was a vague memory. "It's guaranteed to work on those achy bones and open up your stuffy head." Her voice was nice, Tess decided. Kind of like her own mother's voice. Soothing.

She'd set the tray with a bowl of the soup and a glass of orange juice. The cool liquid felt good against her raw throat. She drank half of it. "Nice."

Claire smiled. "Fluids are the key to getting well. Do you think you can try the soup?"

Tess nodded. The soup, too, was soothing.

"Where are Hector and Molly?"

"The dogs?"

Tess nodded.

"Cole took them out for a walk. He said they wouldn't leave your side all morning. But I guess they thought you were okay once you sat up. Dogs are empathetic that way, aren't they? Knowing when things just aren't right?"

Had Cole stayed with her all morning as well?

Claire leaned forward, testing Tess's forehead with the back of her hand. "You're still awfully warm. I prescribe finishing this bowl of soup and lots of rest."

Tess complied, surprisingly weak when she was done.

Claire picked up the tray and put it on the side table.

"Thank you."

"You're welcome."

"And now that rest." Claire helped adjust the pillows.

Tess was losing the struggle against sleep already. "You're berry nice."

Claire tucked the sheets in around her shoulders one final time.

Back in the compact kitchen, she tidied the few dishes and wondered about this woman who'd bailed out her son's company. This woman who made her son want to take care of her, as well.

Cole was back shortly with the dogs, who made a straight line for Tess's bedroom.

"They're very devoted," she commented.

"The Scottie belonged to her brother."

"Oh?"

"He died in Iraq."

"Oh, Cole. Is that why she—"

"It's part of his insurance settlement."

They were quiet for several moments.

"She knows about the vets you hire."

"We drove out to the airport one night."

"Oh?"

The trouble with mothers is that they knew your entire history. "She needed to chill."

"She liked your rehab plan."

"Yeah."

"She seems nice."

Cole considered telling his mother about the missing designs, but she was already worried that he might be deployed again. No need to give her something else to worry about. "Yeah."

"Does she have family?"

He chuckled. "Makes ours look tiny."

"Well, that's good. Did you call her mother?"

"No. I thought I'd wait until after the lunch rush. She's Tess Spencer, Mom. Spencers Restaurants. Her parents run the main restaurant downtown."

Claire immediately glanced down at her casual shirt and pants.

"It's not high tea. You brought over soup. Besides, she's not like that."

"Oh, well," she said with a shrug. "Not much I could do about how I look anyway. Now, I imagine you have to get back to the office."

He nodded.

"I hate to leave her alone."

"Mom!"

"Are you going to call her mother?"

"Guess I am now."

"Then I'll stay until she gets here. She may run a famous restaurant, but she's a mother.

She'll want to check in. If not, then I can make sure Tess has a light supper."

"You have a family of your own."

"Thank you, Cole. I'm aware of that."

Realizing he was being subtly but firmly kicked out, he gave up. He just hoped Tess didn't mind being adopted.

AS SHE GRADUALLY WOKE UP, the murmur of voices reminded Tess of the farmhouse when her aunts would gather. First they would cook and bake. Then they would settle, some would crochet or embroider, but mostly they would talk, that wonderful blend of feminine voices dipping and rising as they exchanged stories and confidences. There was always laughter, and more rarely that softer, teary sadness when the story was painful.

Blinking, Tess came to full consciousness in the warm comfort of her bed. In her town house. Her bedside lamp was on. And a fresh glass of water sat next to her clock. Molly started barking.

The rhythm of the voices broke up.

Judith came into her room. "Hi, honey, how are you feeling?"

"Mom? What are you doing here?"

Her mother stroked her cheeks and forehead. "Better. You're not as warm. Claire's soup must be working."

So Claire wasn't a dream.

"In fact, another bowl of her soup ought to clear up some of that congestion. It was terribly kind of her to make a batch for my little girl."

"Mom—"

"And for Cole to call and let me know how sick you are. You shouldn't try to just keep on going, honey. I like taking care of you. I don't get to do that enough anymore." Judith's eyes filled. "Let me, okay?"

She nodded.

"I'm going to warm up that soup now."

Sandy poked her head in from the doorway. "I don't dare come any farther. I get exposed to at least a zillion germs in the classroom. Just came to make sure you're still kicking."

"Yeth."

"Yowee. I'm definitely staying on this side of the doorway. Besides with two motherly types, you're getting plenty of attention. And we're having fun out here. Claire's great."

"Who's here?"

"Rach, Kate. But they don't want your germs either."

Tess sneezed.

"See how you are? Well, here's your mom with more soup."

Judith brought in a tray and sat on the side of the bed watching Tess eat. "I'm glad you have some appetite. The flu can be wicked."

"It's not so bad," Tess replied, feeling better after some of the steamy liquid.

"You should've called, honey. Cole said you were worried about the restaurants. That's why we have capable assistant managers. I'd much rather be here fussing over you than at the landmark. And meeting Claire is a plus. I don't often get to meet a boyfriend's family. She's a lovely woman."

Tess took another spoonful of soup.

"We'll have to invite the whole family to the restaurant." Judith laughed. "Compared to our *whole* family, there can't be many of them."

Tess dipped her spoon back into the bowl. At this rate the mothers would be planning the wedding by the end of the evening. Then she remembered the check.

And suddenly she felt chilled. Sandy had said he would think she was trying to buy him.

Her mother didn't notice her change in mood as she continued fussing. Tess smiled and nodded as Judith talked, as her cousins called in greetings and when Claire bid her good-night.

But she was worried.

CHAPTER NINE

"THERE'S NO TIME to take a coffee break before submitting Mason's bid," Cole told the design group. "We have their specs. And Mason's already approved the preliminaries."

The designers, mostly young, were bright, handpicked by Jim Frederickson or Cole, before he'd been deployed. He was sure of their talent. Equally sure of his own and Jim's. Now that they had the cash infusion, they also had to make sure the most recent designs stayed in their hands. Nate's team had been working on new security measures.

One man held up his hand. "Garret, isn't it?"

"Yes. What about *our* contracts?"

"Same as before. Renegotiations on your hire date."

"Then we're not going under?" Emily Newsom asked.

"Not today."

The group laughed nervously.

"So we have a good chance with these designs?" Randy asked.

"I think so. Work hard. Work smart. Get this bid, and your bonuses and stock options will show it." Cole hoped his words got through as he left the design department and headed toward security.

There was a new energy vibrating throughout the building. Employees hurrying past him in the halls smiled and greeted him now. He used to feel as though they were trying to escape the executioner.

The security offices weren't glamorous, but then they weren't meant to be. All utilitarian. Computers and cameras. A few desks. High-tech equipment meant to protect the production of high-tech designs.

He knocked on Nate's door.

"Come on in." His desk was spread with reports Cole recognized. "Analyzing badge movements?"

"I'm going over when your computer disappeared. I still can't find anything out of the ordinary. It worries me, Cole. That means it's someone inside."

"Or someone who slipped in unnoticed."

Nate rubbed his jaw. "Could be, but then to get the computer out of your office unseen…"

And into Tess's hands.

"We have to concentrate on *this* batch of designs, Nate. We keep them safe, we're in the clear."

"It's like guarding newly hatched baby birds all wanting to jump out of the nest. Damn it all, Cole. You've got a dozen people with access to the designs."

"A dozen people are working on them, Nate."

"And the designs can walk out of here on one of those little flash point disks the size of my thumb." Nate rubbed his forehead. "Hell, all the designers wear them on cords around their necks. How do you know what they're carrying out of here?"

"Okay. I'll tell Jim to have the designers leave all disks, flash point and otherwise here effective immediately."

"Let's hope they do as instructed."

Cole threw up his hands. "You *want* to frisk them?"

"I'm worried, real worried."

"Yeah." He leaned his head back in the chair. "Yeah."

THE SPEECH Sandy gave to the Women's Literacy Forum was sparkling, fresh, well received. Rachel, Kate and Tess—who'd sponsored a table—applauded along with the rest of the group. Tess, completely recovered from her bout of flu, was glad to be back in the land of the living.

Sandy ducked into her chair. "Was I okay?"

"No, you were fabulous!" Kate gave her more silent applause, tapping her hands lightly together.

"Absolutely!" Tess agreed.

Sandy pulled out her napkin. "I'm glad my part's over. Now I can eat my lunch."

Rachel glanced at her empty plate. "I didn't wait. Sorry. I was starved. If I wait at work I miss out."

"How is work?" Sandy asked.

Rachel shrugged. "Work. Which is all my life is about these days."

Sandy glanced meaningfully at Tess.

"I saw that," Rachel accused. "What was that look about?"

"Just that you haven't met anyone lately," Sandy explained.

"I didn't know you had either," Rachel retorted.

"Nope, but now that Tess has, maybe Cole has friends she can *subtly* set us up with."

Kate rolled her eyes. "That always works."

Tess tapped her fingers on the table.

"What?" Sandy demanded.

"Don't pounce. Cole mentioned he'd like to do something special for the design team since they're working such long hours. What if Spencers catered a fabulous dinner for them, pulled out all the stops?"

"And this would help us meet guys, how?" Rachel asked.

"Three of his executives are single *and* attractive, not to mention the designers themselves, although I think some of them may be a little young. And I can ask him to invite his friend, Allen."

Rachel cleared her throat. "I don't mean to be a stickler on this point—"

"I'll *recruit* you to help out so he won't feel it's an imposition to Spencers."

"Finally," Rachel threw up one hand, "the light."

"We did all work as servers," Kate mused. "So it would be logical to use us."

"And since I'm an investor now it makes perfect sense," Tess added.

"Back up," Rachel said. "What was that?"

"Just that I'm an investor. No big deal."

"Said in that casual tone, it's a big deal. What *have* you done?"

"Rachel, you're my financial advisor, not my mother. I invested in Harrington with some of David's settlement."

She groaned. "Couldn't you have at least run it by me?"

"I made a calculated, informed decision. I did what David would have wanted."

"It's worse than I thought." Rachel sighed. "At least tell me the prospectus isn't in Chinese."

Tess buttered her roll with great care.

"Tess?"

"There's no prospectus, okay?"

Rachel sputtered. "I told you what kind of trouble his company is in. Why would you invest in… Oh, Tess. You did it on purpose! You put your money in his failing business on purpose."

Kate tried to soothe her cousin. "Rach—"

"I can't believe it! I just can't believe it!"

"Well, believe it," Tess snapped. "It was the right thing to do. Sometimes you have to think with your heart. This is what David would've wanted."

"Let's don't forget this is Sandy's special day," Kate reminded them.

Tess and Rachel both glanced guiltily at their cousin.

"I'm sorry," Tess apologized. "I didn't mean to go off like that."

Rachel straightened in her chair. "Actually, I think I'm the one who started it. Sorry."

"It's okay," Sandy replied.

"Could we back up to the part where you might meet someone new?" Tess asked, hoping to coax a smile from Sandy.

"How many of these executive types are single?" Sandy asked cautiously.

"Three. And we can lock Rach in a closet to give you better odds."

Sandy grinned. "Make that Kate, too, and you've got a deal."

They were laughing again, but Tess had a feeling Rachel had latched on to something she wasn't going to give up on. And she'd just invited her into Cole's inner sanctum.

SINCE HE'D DEPOSITED Tess's check, Cole kept waiting for the axe to fall. With each call, fax and e-mail he expected the announcement. But nothing.

Today, however, he'd had a call from Tess. And she said she needed to talk.

Maybe she thought bad news was best delivered in person. The dogs barked when he rang the bell. Once inside, though, they greeted him like an old friend.

"I didn't know you had a cat," Cole said, studying the third member of Tess's menagerie, which looked thin and not nearly as well-manicured as the dogs.

"I don't. Didn't, I mean." Tess smiled. "This little guy was hanging around the garbage cans at the restaurant. You know how manic the traffic is in that area. I was sure he was going to get hit, so I brought him home."

"No collar?"

"Nope. I've called shelters and the SPCA, but no one's reported him missing." She picked up the cat. "I'm taking him to the vet's tomorrow to have him checked over and see if he has a microchip. And a couple of the busboys are going to put up posters."

"What if no one claims him?"

She stroked the cat's fur. "We'll see. So far Molly and Hector are getting along with him. I was worried because Scotties are bred to go after other small animals. But David had a cat when Hector was young and she treated the dog like one of her kittens." She paused. "Would you like some wine?"

He might need the fortification. "Sure."

She put the cat down, but he stayed near her feet. "You're sure this isn't a bad time? We didn't talk long enough on the phone for me to ask if you were busy."

"One time's as good as another."

Tess lifted the bottle, already uncorked, and poured them each a glass of wine. "I've been doing a lot of thinking."

"Oh?"

"It's about something you said when we were discussing the loan."

Cole waited. He'd known it was coming, but he'd wanted so badly to believe in Tess.

"You mentioned veterans' organizations."

His thoughts switched like two high-speed trains approaching the same junction.

"Cole?"

"Yes. The vets' groups."

"Well… I want to do something, but I'm not sure I can deal directly with the vets." Tess cleared her throat. "At least not yet. I keep thinking it would be a good thing to do because of David. But because of David… I don't think I can."

It took Cole a minute. Even after he'd sipped his wine. Even after the relief filtered through his system. "Spencers does a lot of fund-raisers, right?"

She nodded.

"Have a fund-raiser, then donate the proceeds. There are auxiliary organizations for the V.A. hospital. One group helps patients and their families. I know they always need money."

She swirled the wine in her glass. "Do you think I'm being a coward, not being willing to face the men directly?"

Hell, he didn't know what to think about her. "Everybody has to deal with what they can."

"I guess so. Um. I was also thinking about what you mentioned the other day, about doing something special for your design team."

"Yeah."

"I have an idea. Spencers can cater a dinner, the full-out works."

"No! I mean that's too much trouble. I can think of something that's not so—"

"I've already thought it out. We're used to catering. We have everything we need. And I can recruit the girls, my cousins, you know, the ones you met, to help. That way we don't have to use many staff members. It'll be great. We could have a hot buffet and a dessert bar. And we can pull in one of the off-duty bartenders. And you can have your executive staff there so the design team feels really appreciated. Maybe even invite your friend, Allen, isn't that his name? The one from the airport? Kind of a boss's family atmosphere?"

Stunned, Cole couldn't think of anything worse. All of his security measures exposed to Tess and her cousins. Literally putting them in the middle of his operations.

"There wouldn't be room for anything like that in the design department."

"Don't you have a conference room?"

"Of course, but—"

"We could set up there. More practical anyway. Then their work won't be interrupted. We're used to moving our equipment in and out quickly. Think how surprised your employees will be to have a gourmet meal instead of take-out. They'll vote you boss of the year."

"Really, Tess, this is unnecessary."

"It will be my pleasure."

"You've just been sick—"

"And look how you all came to my aid. It's time I paid you back."

He had a sinking feeling that she would.

CHAPTER TEN

TESS HUMMED as she checked over the seafood order.

"It's been a while since I've heard you sound so happy," Judith said, coming up behind her in the huge walk-in cooler.

"It's a beautiful day, don't you think?"

Judith studied her daughter's face. "Yes. As a matter of fact I do. But I didn't think you were noticing that sort of thing much lately."

"It's just that it's especially nice today."

"Then I'm glad."

"Mom?"

"Yes?"

"Wasn't it awful when Dad went to war?"

"Yes."

"I'm sorry."

"It was difficult when your dad was gone. And when David left."

And never came home.

"Tess, when your brother was deployed, I had a bad feeling."

"You never told me that!"

"And make you worry even more? No. You could call it maternal instinct, but in my heart I knew."

Tess hugged her mother close.

Blinking back her tears, Judith pulled herself together. "Now, about *your* young man. He seems special."

Tess suddenly felt as if she were sixteen, talking about one of her dates. "Really?"

"Really. How about filling me in?"

So Tess did. "Sandy thinks I shouldn't have offered him the loan."

"It's a funny thing. When we're in trouble we'll accept help from our friends without thought. But money…" Judith shook her head. "I've never understood why people will accept money from strangers but not their friends. And if a loan will save his business, why not? It's only a barrier if you let it become one."

"I hope David would approve. I think he would."

"Tess, you have good instincts. Trust them."

"I'm trying. I was talking to Cole last night and he suggested a fund-raiser here at the landmark Spencers for one of the veteran's hospital auxiliary groups. What do you think?"

"An excellent idea." Judith paused. "Except…"

Tess waited.

"Honey, you've been working so many hours as it is. I hate to see you take on any more projects."

"I was thinking of roping in the girls to help."

"Now, that's a good idea. If you'll really delegate…"

"You know how they are. I'll be lucky to even know what's going on after the three of them take over."

Judith checked her watch. "I've got to call the florist. My order changed again."

As her mother left, Tess turned her thoughts to the other party—the one for Cole's design group. Simultaneously setting up her three cousins. Now that would be a first.

UNABLE TO STOP the Tess Blitzkrieg, Cole enlisted security to tighten the hatches during the surprise dinner. Nate and Jim were put on special alert. All the adjoining offices to the conference room were locked. The entire design department was shut and locked down. Only one entrance and exit were made available for the catering crew. Cole figured that with the shutdown time he could have ferried his design team to Spencers and purchased their finest entrees, but he couldn't tell Tess that without revealing his lack of trust.

The stewards that rolled the trolleys off the catering vans were professional, and in an amazingly short time the conference room resembled a fine dining room with crisp linen, crystal, china, silver and huge bouquets of flowers. And true to Tess's word, her cousins were there to serve.

Cole's employees were bowled over by the whole dog and pony show. Many of them had never even been on an expense account before, so this was prime treatment.

The food, as promised, was fabulous, the service exceptional. Sandy, Rachel and Kate circulated around the room with appetizer and drink trays. Others kept the buffet refilled, attended to the bar.

The party atmosphere was contagious. Cole

noticed that even his executives were mellowing. But he groaned when he spotted Rachel zeroing in on Jim. Just like a piranha, she went after the gentlest fish in the tank. Not that Jim would ever give up any of their secrets, still…

Randy, one of several young designers surrounding Cole, held up his glass. "Great party, Cole!"

"Can we put a monthly party like this in the new contract?" Garret asked. "Guaranteed to boost productivity."

"I'll keep that in mind."

Garret grinned as a steward uncovered a dessert bar. He and Randy moved in that direction. It really was an amazing spread.

Emily, one of the youngest designers, caught his attention. "Cole, when I was hired, Allen said the company had a family atmosphere. I couldn't imagine it. But this tonight…well, it's really nice."

"When I founded Harrington, that's what I wanted."

She smiled shyly. "My dad told me how important it is to work for a place that puts people first like this, that it matters more than salary or benefits because your job is where you spend most of your time. Well, anyway, thanks."

"Thanks for the hard work, Emily."

"Sure."

For all the nerve-racking pressure the evening had caused, there was this, the clear benefit. And as the evening wound down he could see that everybody seemed relaxed, revived.

As the stewards packed up, leaving out the bar and desserts, Tess handed Cole a tiny, impossibly dark cup of coffee. "Don't worry. It's spiked."

"In that case..." he accepted the cup "...thanks."

He watched a steward wheel out a trolley, saw that a security guard was casually monitoring the movement.

"...okay?"

Distracted, Cole pulled his attention back to Tess. "Sorry?"

"Is something wrong?"

"I'm just amazed you could transform our boring conference room into a dinner party."

Tess smiled. "It's not the first time we've done this. So, you think it was a success?"

"The team really liked it."

"Everyone enjoys being spoiled. And when they're working hard, they like to know the effort's noticed, appreciated."

"They sure do."

Tess was dressed in a crisp white shirt and black linen trousers like the other servers. It certainly didn't make her look like a corporate spy. He took another swallow from the tiny cup. Relaxed and joking, Tess appeared sincere, real. He noticed that she even had a dimple when she smiled. He drained his drink. Spiked with what? He didn't need to go soft now.

But he'd taken precautions. Nate had installed cameras in the conference room and hallway. If anybody strayed from the designated areas, they had it on one of the tapes. Security was going to review them once the event was over.

Jim bumped into him. "Sorry, Cole. But hey, looks like the evening's gone well."

Cole glanced at Tess. "Thanks to our hostess."

"I'm going to give Rachel a ride home," Jim said. "See you in the morning."

Cole stared after them. It couldn't have been Kate or Sandy who latched on to Jim. It had to be Rachel.

People trickled out until only one steward remained, and he packed the bar into the loaded van.

Cole walked with Tess to the parking lot. "Thanks for putting this together."

"My pleasure. Remember, I'm an investor now."

Not something he was likely to forget. "It was really impressive, Tess."

"Well, I'll say good night." The words were barely out of her mouth as the van drove off.

"That was good timing," she said with a small, embarrassed laugh. "I guess Jason didn't realize I was supposed to be riding back with him. The girls and I rode here with a different guy, the same one Kate and Sandy rode back with. Mixed signals."

He chuckled. "The steward's loss. I'm parked right over here."

COLE WALKED Tess to the door of her town house and waited while she unlocked and opened the door. Her dogs rushed to greet her, then Molly pushed past to greet him as well.

Tess bent over automatically to pick up her mail. As Cole scratched Molly's wiggling body, he noticed Tess stiffen. She was staring at an envelope.

"Something wrong?"

It took her a moment to reply. "It's from David's unit in Iraq."

Corralling the dogs, he pushed the door shut and guided Tess inside. "Come on."

She clutched the letter, allowing him to guide her to the sofa.

"Do you want to open it?"

She stared at the standard issue stationery the soldiers used. "It can't be any worse news. He can't be any more dead than he already is." Tears fell at odds with the words.

She'd just been laughing. Not that it mattered, he knew. One of his unit's worst losses had been much the same. After getting mail, they'd been in particularly good humor. And then an RPG made a direct hit, killing one man, wounding two others.

It seemed natural to put his arms around her, to hold her close. She was soft in his arms, this strong-minded woman.

"You'd have liked David, I think." Her voice struggled, breaking between the words, but he could tell she needed to talk about him. "He thought a lot like you do." She sniffled as she tried to laugh. "But we didn't fight about it." She rested her head on Cole's shoulder. "He was so good for our family, always looking out for the cousins—not just the ones you met. I have some who wanted to make restauranting their careers—Eric and Joseph—and David encouraged them. And he took such an interest in everyone. And…" She crumpled, crying silently. Cole could feel the tears soaking his shirt.

He rubbed her back as quiet sobs shook her body. Releasing the gold fastener that held her hair up in a knot, he smoothed her hair loose, trying to absorb some of the shock she felt at seeing the letter.

Her crying subsided gradually. "I'm sorry," she said shakily. "I—"

"There's nothing to be sorry for."

"I miss him so much."

"I know."

Her eyes lifted, darkening to indigo. How had he missed that they could do that? He stroked her cheek with the back of his fingers.

Her skin was soft. He forgot about rushing back to the office, about security tapes, about their differences. Instead he kept her nestled by his side as she talked about David.

Cole didn't try to keep track of time. He uncorked one of her bottles of wine and when she was ready, they opened the letter together. From one of the men who'd served with David, it spoke of what a great guy he'd been, how he was missed.

For a long time she held the thin pages of paper, creasing and recreasing them. "You know, sometimes, when I first wake up in the morning, I forget. Just for a minute. And then I remember. And I wonder if it'll always be like that."

Cole refilled her wineglass. "Do you remember his smile?"

She nodded.

"You'll always remember that."

She creased the letter one more time, then laid it down. "Yeah?"

"Yeah."

She slipped her hand into his. The night lengthened as she told him about David, about his dreams. A silent truce declared, he listened as she told him about an upbringing and life that made him question how he could even think she'd be involved in the theft. Besides, a thief wouldn't return the goods. Would she?

"THAT'S THE LAST ONE." Nate pulled the security tape from the previous night.

Cole sat back in his chair. "Nothing."

"And none of my men saw anything suspicious. Just a party."

No reason to suspect Tess had an ulterior reason for setting this up. "Did you see Jim leave with Rachel De Villard?"

"Why?"

"I don't trust her."

"You don't think Jim—"

"Of course not." Cole pressed his palms to his head. "And there weren't any breaches of the design department?"

"Not one."

"Good."

"You don't sound relieved."

"I am." Unless the party wasn't to take something out, but to bring someone in. Rachel. So she could meet Jim. Then he thought of Tess the previous evening. He didn't believe she'd faked her behavior.

But was Rachel using her? If so, Tess probably didn't suspect it. It would explain why she'd returned his computer. Why she'd offered to loan him the money. It sure as hell wasn't going to be easy to find out.

"We done here?"

Cole nodded. "Nate?"

"Yes?"

"Nothing." No one else was going to be able to help him with this one.

"THANKS AGAIN for volunteering at Cole's party," Tess said to her cousins.

"It was fun," Kate replied.

"Even though Rachel *benefited* the most," Sandy added.

Tess laughed. "She did seem to zoom right in on Jim Frederickson."

"Where is she?"

"She couldn't get away from work."

They were working on the fund-raiser for the veterans' hospital auxiliary. Kate was in her element. She loved parties and she loved planning them. Sandy was her right-hand go-to person. Rachel, being Rachel, had contributed her Rolodex of heavy hitters.

"I've had twenty-seven more replies," Kate announced. "Rachel's Rolodex is mining gold."

"At fifteen hundred dollars a plate, you've got that right," Tess agreed.

"And, Tess, you should meet the women in

this auxiliary." Sandy studied Kate's list. "They're an incredible group of volunteers."

"I'm sure they are." But seeing the wounded soldiers in person was something she still couldn't bear.

"Sandy's right. Some of the patients in the V.A. hospital don't have *anyone*. Either their families live too far away from Houston or they're all alone. I can't imagine going to war, getting wounded and then coming home to find no one cares." Kate finished with a gasp, turning to Tess. "I'm sorry! That just slipped out."

"It's okay. You're right. It's a terrible thing."

"I have some good news," Sandy announced, changing the subject. "Cole agreed to be one of the speakers at the fund-raiser."

Tess choked on her Diet Coke. "Who asked him to speak?"

"Me." Kate's doe-eyed expression seemed unexpectedly as though it might have the power to crush any and all opposition. "Wasn't that okay?"

"I'm just surprised," Tess assured her. "I'm sure he'll be an interesting speaker."

Sandy winked. "And he'll look great at the lectern."

Tess ignored her. "So, how many people have responded so far?"

"With these twenty-seven, my count's over one hundred and fifty so far."

Tess stared at her.

Kate checked the figures on her notepad. "No, that's not right."

Of course not.

"It's more like one hundred and eighty."

"Really?" Tess was astonished. "Wow."

"Patriotism's still strong," Sandy reminded her. "I'm sure you must be happy about that."

"I'd be more pleased if all our soldiers were coming home."

"I think we all would," Sandy said quietly.

Kate glanced down at the invitations, pushing them into a pile. "No one wants them over there, Tess."

"But they're still there."

"Holding this fund-raiser, doesn't that help? I mean, we're doing what we can to help on this end, right?" Kate asked. "And we have to support the soldiers still over there, don't we?"

Sandy nodded. "I think so, too."

Tess glanced at both of them. "It's so complicated. I'm not saying I don't support our troops. I'm saying bring them home."

"Agreed," Sandy said. "Now, can we get back to the fund-raiser?"

"On one condition. You'll both help me stuff envelopes and raise money for Families of the Fallen."

"Done." Kate and Sandy replied in unison.

Kate checked her notepad again "FYI, Tess, your mom had us send Cole's family complimentary invitations to the fund-raiser."

"She told me she wanted to have his whole family over," Tess groaned.

"A little early for that?" Sandy sympathized.

"*Way* early."

Kate grinned. "Problem solved."

IT HAD BEEN a horrendous day. Everything that could go wrong did. The fish order never arrived. They were three servers short. And Tess would've caught the errors but she'd been at the landmark location making preparations for the upcoming fund-raiser. She was just too stretched.

As Tess rechecked the Galleria restaurant dining room for more gaffes, she saw Cole making his way toward her. She had been looking forward to seeing him, but not now, not when she was so rushed.

"Cole."

"You're busy."

"Well, yes, actually I am. It's been… well—"

"I'll come back tonight. I take it you'll still be here?"

"Oh, yes."

"Later, then."

"See you."

He started to leave.

"Cole? Thanks."

The assistant manager rushed up just then. In the distraction, Cole departed.

It was literally hours before Tess could think about him again. The dinner and after-theater crowds had thinned and only the occasional tables were filled.

But now, instinct caused her to head toward the bar. The jazz quartet's music had softened with the lengthening of the night. Couples sat close at intimate tables and the subdued lighting glinted off spotless glasses. Following her internal compass, Tess honed in on Cole, who sat at a table alone.

For a moment her breath stuttered. Alone and waiting for her. How was it she felt the heat before she even reached him?

Then he was standing, his gaze holding hers. "Tess."

"Hi." She chose the chair angled close to his and when he sat she felt his leg graze hers. Her throat was dry; her thoughts scattered.

"Did I wait long enough?"

She smiled. "This is my favorite time at the restaurant. It's quiet, almost thoughtful." She shook her head. "I suppose that doesn't sound very businesslike."

"Not everything's about the bottom line."

She grinned. "I'll have to remind you of that when you're buried in paperwork at the plant."

He lifted his glass. "Actually I'm here about business."

The disappointment nearly crushed her. "Oh?"

"Partially. We never figured out whether your money should be a loan or an investment."

"I want to do the right thing. Would an investment be all right with you?"

His beautiful blue eyes were hard to read in the low light. "Fine."

She hated when someone said "fine." It was so noncommittal. "What was the other reason you're here?"

"To see you. How'd the crisis turn out?"

She smiled again, the crush in her chest easing. "I don't remember calling it a crisis."

"I read between the lines."

"You don't want to hear all this," she protested.

"Try me."

She detailed everything that had gone wrong, then smiled wryly. "So I was a bit frantic when I saw you earlier."

"There's a solution."

Tess remembered his earlier suggestion, to bring in another manager. "I told you, it's not that easy."

"The hard decisions never are."

"Family's so important to Dad."

"And you have a huge one," he reminded her.

"But they're not Spencers."

"They're still family, aren't they? The ones you told me about, Eric and Joseph?"

Tess didn't want to get choked up again around him. "It's difficult to face…this truth… that David won't ever be coming back. Logically, I know that. But my heart…it doesn't want to give up hope yet."

He caressed the back of her head. "And you shouldn't. That's David in your heart, where he'll always be."

She tried hard. Damned hard. But a tear made it past her determination. "I'm sorry. I keep doing this."

He pulled her close. There weren't any certain words that he needed to say, or she needed to hear. But as he sat with her in the favorite hour and favorite part of her restaurant, she heard them. All of them.

CHAPTER ELEVEN

THE LARGEST banquet room at the landmark Spencers covered the entire second floor. And yet the room was crowded for Tess's fund-raiser. Of course, not everyone who purchased tickets actually showed up, but there was still an impressive turnout. And Tess had all the details of the party under control.

Still, she felt nervous until she'd finally met the rest of Cole's family. She immediately liked his father, a quiet, older version of Cole, still handsome. It was interesting to see the Harringtons all mingling well with her parents. Claire and her mother acted like old friends. She hadn't known women could bond over chicken soup. Maybe it was a generational thing.

Tess scanned the room for Cole. At first she almost didn't recognize him. He was wearing his uniform.

As he approached she continued to stare. "Tess."

"Hi."

"Kate asked me to wear the uniform."

Tess cleared her throat. "Oh."

"Because I'm speaking."

"Sure."

"Tess? You all right?"

"Just surprised." She looked away. "I met your family over there. Of course you have to sit at the head table, but—"

"Tess, it's a uniform. Nothing more."

"Which you're very attached to."

"Granted."

"The last time I saw one wasn't under the best circumstances."

He clenched his teeth. "Tess, my talk tonight—"

Kate abruptly stepped between them and took his arm. "Cole, I'm so glad you're here. Several sponsors would like to meet you, especially some of the corporate patrons. Tess, you don't mind if I borrow him, do you?"

She shook her head, then watched them circulate through the room. He seemed to be saying all the right things, impressing all the right people. But all she could see was the uniform.

Then it was time to take her place at the speakers' table. She began by acknowledging Kate and Sandy, who in turn introduced Cole.

Sandy smiled in his direction as she rose. "We're fortunate tonight to have as our first guest speaker a respected member of our business community, the CEO and founder of Harrington Engineering. As a member of the armed services, recently returned from Iraq, he has a special bond with our cause tonight. Because he was wounded himself, Cole spent time in one of the hospitals that are filled with servicemen and women. Veterans of all U.S. wars and conflicts from the past and present century are patients in Houston's regional veterans' hospital. Members of the women's auxiliary make their stay a better one, bridging the gap between family and income. Sometimes, by simply being a friend. It is my honor to introduce Captain Cole Harrington."

Applause broke out as people stood to welcome him. But Tess was having trouble catching her breath. Wounded? Cole had been wounded. He hadn't said anything. Hadn't indicated that he could've returned as David had. In a box.

Cole's first words slipped by her as he thanked the audience, Spencers, Tess and her cousins.

As she imagined him being wounded.

It took a few moments for her to be able to hear what he was saying.

When she did, she felt even worse. He spoke of a young man from New York City who survived the attack on 9/11, then joined the Army. That young man had been in his command, Cole explained, and had been killed by an insurgent's car bomb.

The audience was silent, absorbed by his tale. Tess felt the blow of his words, the horror Cole had experienced.

Cole continued by telling them how proud the young man's family would have been. But his parents and sister who ran a store beneath the Twin Towers hadn't survived. So it was up to the ordinary citizens to honor him, to keep alive the patriotism he had believed in to the end.

The emotional address was met with a standing ovation.

Tess's legs were shaky as she stood. It seemed to take forever for the applause to die, for people to settle down enough for her to introduce the next speaker.

She prayed that her voice wouldn't be as shaky as her legs. "I know we're all very grateful to…" she couldn't bring herself to call him captain "…to Cole for bringing the reality to us. In that vein, our next guest, Susan Johnson, is here to speak on behalf of the local chapter of Families of the Fallen." She ignored Cole's startled expression as she sat.

Susan Johnson's twenty-year-old son had lost a leg in Iraq. He had gone from playing football to enlisting in a burst of patriotic spirit. He'd always dreamed of an athletic career, but that had ended when a land mine took his leg. Now he faced an uncertain future.

After listening to both speakers, people began offering to increase their donations. Kate and Sandy circulated with the auxiliary officers, gratefully accepting checks.

"Tess." Sandy snagged her by the arm. "This is Nancy Carter, president of the auxiliary."

"Ms. Spencer, this fund-raiser has been beyond our wildest dreams. And now, tonight, well…I don't know how to thank you."

"Call me Tess, please. And the credit goes to Mr. Harrington and my cousins, Sandy and Kate."

"I'm very grateful to you all. This donation will make a world of difference to our patients."

Sandy smiled. "It shouldn't take us long to tally up the net proceeds."

"That won't be necessary," Tess said impulsively. "Spencers will absorb the expenses. Consider it our contribution."

Sandy's eyes widened and Nancy gasped.

"Thank you so much. We're so grateful," Nancy replied. "I can't wait for you to visit the hospital, see the difference the money you've raised makes."

When Tess didn't speak, Sandy smoothed over the moment. "I'd like to come along."

"Perfect," Nancy replied. She grasped Tess's hands. "There's nothing as gratifying as seeing your donation in action."

Tess swallowed, unable to refuse. "That would be wonderful."

They walked away and Tess shook hands with more guests, accepting congratulations for bringing attention to the cause.

During a brief lull, she felt the hair on her neck prickle and she knew Cole was near.

Then he was facing her. "You didn't tell me about the other speaker."

She touched the purple heart on his chest, still upset from hearing he'd been wounded. "You had a few surprises of your own."

"You want to talk about this here?"

Not with both of their families in the same room. "I'll be home in about an hour."

COLE KNEW he could take the confrontation to the next level. Instead he swung by his house, changed into jeans and, on impulse, rode his motorcycle to Tess's.

When he arrived, she had changed as well and was out in her courtyard. "Getting ready to walk the dogs?"

"No. My walker already did."

"Want to go for a ride then?"

"Okay."

Tess whistled when she saw the gleaming Harley.

He handed her a helmet.

Out on the road, he leaned into the curves, and Tess held on, pressing into his back. He kicked the bike into gear, letting it take them through the darkness. He kept to the back roads where he had control. He needed control right then. Something Tess didn't understand. He hadn't served his country so he could apologize for it.

He was still angry when he eventually slowed the cycle. Gravel spit up from the tires as he pulled off onto a grassy slope.

Tess slipped off the back of the bike. "Were you hurt badly?"

Dismounting, he shook his head.

She placed a hand on his shoulder. "Would you tell me if you were?"

The heat of his anger shifted. Pulling off a glove, he traced his fingers over her lips. Her questioning eyes undid him.

It started out as a tentative kiss, but somewhere between thought and action, it changed, took on a force of its own.

Her lips were tender, meeting his, scattering his senses. He felt her tremble and that barest motion whispered against his skin, knocked him off balance.

He pulled her closer, needing to feel all of her against him, needing more than a taste. More than the tangle of her hair in his fisted hands. Her cotton shirt and trousers were deceptively seductive, and he felt the crush of her breasts against his chest, the contours of her hips as they pressed against his.

She trailed her hands over his throat, a scorching torment, then ran them over his shoulders and finally his back. He could imagine those same sensations against bare skin and wanted to see if it would be as fine as he imagined.

Her heart thudded against his, an erratic beat that told him he might just wake in the morning with the tousle of her dark hair on his chest.

Pulling back a fraction, he took in her closed eyes, flushed skin, swollen lips.

"Tess?"

"Yes?" Her voice was low, her breathing audibly uneven.

He swallowed against temptation. They were standing on the side of the road. "We'd better get back on the bike."

"Um."

"And head back."

Her expression—her eyes—was still languid. "Oh?"

Unable to resist, he nipped at her inviting lower lip. "Unless we want to be the roadside show."

The wind still seemed hot as they rode back to Tess's town house. In her courtyard, she slipped her hand in his. "I'm glad you changed out of your uniform."

"You'll only see it on Reserves weekends."

"Reserves?"

"Army Reserves. Nothing out of the ordinary."

"Nothing?" Her face was suddenly pale.

"Tess?"

"You already served. Why do you have to go on training weekends?"

"I'm still in the Reserves."

"When were you planning to tell me this?"

"I assumed you knew. I'd barely gotten back from deployment when we met. That means I'm active Reserves. I have another year to this hitch."

"Then you're done? For good?"

He hesitated. "Tess…"

"It's not over, is it?"

"I don't want to lie to you. I've been planning to reenlist."

She jerked her hand away. "Why? Why would you do that?"

How could he make her understand it was the right thing to do? "It's complicated."

"No. It's very simple. You could die!"

"Tess—"

"I can't believe you let me care about you, knowing—" her breath grew short "—knowing you could get called up again."

She turned away but he could see the start of tears.

"Tess—"

"Why?"

"I…"

She shook her head, her eyes dark. Then she went inside, shutting the door behind her. Instinctively he knew this was worse than anything else he could've put between them.

THE VETERAN HOSPITAL'S massive granite complex was spread out over more than a hundred acres. Designed in four sections with four atriums, its layout seemed intimidating to the unfamiliar.

The huge parking lots were all full, suggesting that the buildings would be as well. Trees shaded portions of the landscaped exterior, bolstered by big terra cotta pots of bright flowers and evergreens.

As they approached the entrance, she saw patients using crutches or sitting in wheelchairs, many motorized. Men and women of all ages were going in and out.

"These must be the outpatients Nancy told us about," Sandy whispered.

Tess nodded, still astounded by the size of the facility. They must treat a lot of patients.

The lobby was full. Some outpatients were even perched on large circular planters as they waited. Tess hoped she could go through with this.

Nancy approached them before she could back out. "Welcome."

Sandy pocketed her keys. "Thanks for meeting us out here."

Nancy grinned. "I didn't want you to get lost."

Sandy stared down the long, wide hallways. "This place is huge. I had no idea."

"We outgrew our original location more than ten years ago. Wars end, but care for the wounded and disabled doesn't."

Promoting that message was one of the reasons Tess worked with Families of the Fallen.

Nancy took them on a tour of the common

areas, stopping at one of the physical therapy units. Tess watched the patients struggling to regain their mobility. How would David have coped if fate had sent him here?

A young man who appeared to be severely burned over his whole body grinned and joked with his therapist. Tess and Sandy exchanged glances. How could he be so cheerful?

Nancy didn't linger, guiding them through what seemed like one maze after another. Tess would never be able to find her way to the exit on her own. There were numerous sets of elevators, halls that zigzagged in every direction.

Nancy paused at a large, glassed-in room. "There's a similar space on every floor. Our group uses the rooms to play bingo. The prizes aren't expensive, but they make playing more fun. It's just one of the events we sponsor. Because we're a regional hospital, a lot of patients don't have family close enough to visit. We try to fill in the gap. And sometimes, providing just the small things like toiletries or books makes a difference."

"Why do patients come to regional hospitals instead of ones in their own towns?" Sandy asked.

"Most of the smaller hospitals have been shut down—budget cutbacks—so they don't have a choice."

Tess didn't realize until Nancy had led them farther that they were now in a hallway of patient rooms. It made her uneasy. "I don't want to disturb anyone."

"We're just passing through," Nancy assured her.

Tess wanted to look away but she couldn't. Some of the beds were occupied by men old enough to be her grandfather, others David's age or younger. The tug on her heart was palpable.

"Do most of them get visitors?" Sandy asked.

"Some. The oldest patients often don't have anyone left or their spouses aren't able enough to visit on their own."

Tess wanted to make it better for each one of the patients she saw. "But your volunteers visit with them?"

"As much as possible. We're spread pretty thin throughout the hospital. There've been so many federal funding cuts, volunteers are assuming duties that used to be paid."

"Why isn't that on the news?" Sandy asked.

"Families of the Fallen is trying to get the message out," Tess explained. "Nancy, I didn't think I could do it, but I want to volunteer."

"That's great." At that moment, the woman's pager beeped. "I need to take this. Would you excuse me for a few minutes?"

"We didn't have to come here today," Sandy said after Nancy left.

"It was already set up." Tess shrugged. "And if I hadn't come today, I probably never would."

Sandy's face was shadowed with worry. "I wish you'd talk to Cole, give him a chance to explain."

"There's nothing to explain."

"Of course there is. Tess, I don't believe for a minute that he wants to hurt you. Maybe this Reserves issue is something you can work out."

"He wants to be in the Reserves, period. So, there's nothing else to say."

"You've been happier since he came into your life. And don't try to deny it."

The ache Tess felt was familiar, yet different. She carried it with her, unable to shake it, even less able to stop thinking about Cole. "Why didn't he tell me?"

Sandy touched her arm. "I can't imagine why

he'd bring up the subject of the Reserves knowing how sensitive it is for you."

"He could be deployed tomorrow." The thought of him serving again, being wounded again, or worse… She couldn't breathe.

"Would you care for him less? Would you be able to turn away and not know if he was all right?"

Tess fought back her tears. Damn him.

She knew her causes weren't in conflict. She'd never been against her own country or its soldiers. Just seeing them die.

CHAPTER TWELVE

TESS RUBBED Molly's ears, accepting the dog's kisses in return. She reached for Hector just as the doorbell rang, startling her, and sending the dogs in a barking frenzy toward the front door.

Peering through the peephole, Tess saw that it was Cole. She opened the door. "Hi."

"You talking to me?"

She didn't meet his eyes. "I was just going to take the dogs for a walk."

"Want some company?"

"Okay."

They left the town house by way of the French doors that led out back to her abbreviated courtyard. Despite its small size, it was a charming space. A Victorian-style gaslight cast a soft glow on the cobblestone terrace. And a wrought iron bistro table and two chairs, tucked beneath the tall fronds of a banana tree, looked invitingly relaxing.

The town house was set back in a wooded area carved out of what used to be forest. Tall streetlamps lit the manicured lawn, which was thick and soft beneath their feet. The dogs took off sniffing along the familiar route from the backyard to the street.

"I figured you knew about the Reserves, being active I mean."

"If I'd thought it out, I would have. And knowing how you feel, I guess I should've figured out that you'd reenlist, too."

"Can you understand why?"

Her throat tightened. "Why you might go back and die in a war we can't possibly win? No, I can't." She bit her cheek hard so she wouldn't give in to tears.

Suddenly Hector and Molly barked furiously at the bushes they were passing.

"Probably a raccoon," Tess murmured. "Come on, guys." She tugged on Molly's leash. "You'll wake everyone in the neighborhood."

Reluctantly the dogs obeyed and they continued walking, reaching the quiet path that led to the park.

Cole glanced at her. "It was a good thing you did, sponsoring the fund-raiser."

"I went out there. To the hospital."

For a few moments there was nothing but the sound of their footsteps and the dogs rooting through the grass. "How was it?"

"There was a man there, a boy really, who survived a car bomb. I wanted to meet him because I thought about the boy you talked about, and I thought, wouldn't it have been wonderful if he'd survived."

"Tess, you don't have to—"

"But when I got to his room, I found out there wasn't much left of him. His brother told me that when the bomb detonated, it split him open like a watermelon. It took both his arms and wrecked his spine. Somehow he's still alive. And I couldn't help thinking it wasn't going to be much of a life, what's left of it. He's nineteen. Nineteen! This is what *I'm* protesting, Cole. More boys winding up like him. It's what we don't see on the nightly news." She stopped suddenly to face him. "You didn't even tell me you were wounded."

"Why should that change anything? It happened and now it's over."

Moonlight supplemented the soft glow of the streetlights, allowing him to see her troubled eyes. "But I need to—"

"Move on," he said quietly.

"I'm not ready to forget anything."

"There's a difference between the two."

"I wish people would quit telling me how to think!"

Ignoring the tangle of leashes, he pulled her close. "Tess, it *will* get better. I promise." He kissed the smooth skin of her forehead, her cheek, and held her until her breathing calmed.

Hector started digging, pulling on his leash and dragging Molly along with him. After unwinding the leashes, he and Tess continued their walk, finally circling back.

He badly wanted to come back inside with her, but he could tell she needed to be alone. Still, he wished she didn't seem quite so lonely as she shut the door behind her with a clang. It took him a moment before he could turn away and walk back to his car.

COLE PICKED UP the new financials. "Dan?"

"The loan made the difference. It shored up

accounts payable and our R&D budget. It's all there in the forecast."

"Any improvement yet on receivables?"

"Minimal."

Cole nodded. "Mark, continue to keep things tight. Hiring freeze stays unless cleared by me. I want you to personally sign off on all requisitions and purchase orders. I don't want to order one extra pencil we don't need right now."

"Got it. We'll hold steady."

But if they didn't plug the leak, that could change, too. "Nate, security report."

"No changes. Badge data analysis is consistent. We've upped the night shift for both the office and the plant."

Cole swivelled in Jim's direction. "And the million dollar question…"

"Designs are right on track."

"And your team's leaving all disks in the department, not taking them off premises?"

"As instructed."

"All right, guys, that's it for now."

Cole stopped Jim before he could leave with the others.

"What's up?"

"That's what I was going to ask you."

Jim's expression was puzzled.

"About Rachel."

Jim's face cleared. "She's great. I've never met anyone quite like her."

"She's unique."

Jim's smile widened. "You'd know—because of Tess. I mean at first, I thought, wow, she's some talker. And I'm not sure I can keep up with her, you know, being such a big financial player. But there's a lot more to her than that."

"Yeah."

Slowly the other man's smile faded. "What's with you?"

"Just that I'm not sure you know Rachel as well as you think you do."

Jim drew his eyebrows together. "And you do?"

"Don't you think she zeroed in on you pretty fast?"

Jim shoved the chair that stood between them halfway across the room. "You're way over the line!"

"We've been friends a long time—"

"Don't make me forget that. Rachel's none of your damned business."

Cole watched him storm out of the office. Well, he'd blown that. Not that he was sure what he should've said. *Watch that pillow talk. Make sure Rachel doesn't get away with our designs. She's on her way to a full partnership. If Alton's one of her clients, what better way to make sure she makes it?*

If he had that kind of nerve, he'd confront Tess, tell her about his suspicions toward Rachel himself. Maybe he should. It'd been two weeks since he'd seen her. He'd tried to give her time. But his impatience was growing.

He glanced at his watch. A quick call to the restaurant told him Tess wasn't there. Maybe she was volunteering at the hospital.

He hadn't been out to the regional center since his return. As he walked through the wide loading and unloading area in the driveway, he saw older vet volunteers helping outpatients into vans. Part of the brotherhood Tess would never understand.

The big circular information desk was staffed by one of the women who recognized him from the fund-raiser.

"Yes, Tess is here." The woman consulted a sheet. "She's on 3-B North. Do you need someone to show you the way?"

"No, I can find it. Thanks." The otherwise

plain walls were filled with presidential por-
traits, pictures of specific units. He recognized
the Tuskegee Airmen and a tribute to the Navajo
windtalkers.

Vets of all ages filled the busy hallways. It
was sobering to see how many there were. After a few wrong turns, he reached the elevator.
There were so many sets of elevators and halls
he still wasn't sure he was at the right one.

A man in a wheelchair waited off to the side.

"Do these go to 3-North?"

"That's what I'm told."

Cole quickly saw the man was blind. "Sorry.
Didn't realize."

There were Braille signs low on the walls
and markers on the elevators buttons. The man's
loss of sight must be so recent he didn't know
how to read them yet.

"It's okay."

"Are you going up?"

"Yeah."

"I can take you," Cole offered. "Unless you
have to wait for someone."

"Don't want to take you out of your way."

"I'm going there anyway. I'm looking for
my…friend, Tess. She's a volunteer here."

"She's been coming to the unit the past two weeks?"

Cole was surprised the man would know that since he must interact with dozens of people in the hospital. "Yes, that's right."

"She and Mary talk quite a bit."

"Mary?"

"She's my…she was my fiancée."

"I'm Cole Harrington by the way."

"Ron Sinclair."

"Good to meet you, Ron."

"Did Mary ask you to talk to me?"

"No." For a few moments there was just the uncomfortable sound of the elevator rising. "I was deployed with the Reserves," Cole finally said. "You?"

"Reserves, too."

"Iraq?"

"Yes."

They got off the elevator at the third floor. "What'd you do in civilian life?"

"Software engineer."

"That's my business, too."

"You anything to do with Harrington Engineering?" Ron asked.

"Guilty."

"You're a legend."

"You wouldn't say that if you knew the shape my business is in. Where are we heading on this floor?"

"My room'll work. 323."

"Some of the guys are in the big room here."

"That's okay."

Cole belatedly realized Ron wouldn't get much out of watching television or playing games. Together they found the room. The first bed was empty, neatly made. Ironically, Ron's was the one nearest the window.

"Have you been back long?"

"Six months. Germany, Walter Reed, here." Ron's tone wasn't bitter, just defeated.

"What's the prognosis?"

"My back's a lot better, leg too. But my sight…" He hesitated only briefly, his voice flat. "It's not going to improve."

"That's rough. I was lucky. Wounded, but no permanent disability. Some of the guys in my unit didn't make it. It's still hard for me to deal with. Well…you know how it is."

"I do."

Glancing at his watch, Cole shook his head. "I guess I'd better try to find Tess before it gets any later. I'm afraid she'll leave before I see her. It was good speaking with you, Ron."

"That's it? No sermon on how blindness shouldn't affect my life?"

"How would I know about that? Like I said, my wounds didn't leave any lasting effects. I'd be lying if I said I know how you feel, or how you're going to cope."

Ron swallowed hard.

Cole thought of his advice to Tess. "If you wouldn't mind, I'd like to visit again."

There was a short silence. "That'd be okay."

"It was good meeting you."

As he left the room, Cole sensed the other man's unseeing eyes following him. He could only imagine how it felt to be locked in his darkness.

COLE DIDN'T FIND TESS. He searched all over the huge third floor. The halls extended in a giant wagon wheel. Just as he thought he'd exhausted the search, he realized the hall jutted out in another direction.

And, in the end, he decided it was just as well he didn't find her. She hadn't gotten past his commitment to the Reserves. It wouldn't be the best timing to let her know his suspicions about Rachel.

And Ron had reaffirmed his feeling that his commitment was the right thing to do. When Cole had been deployed, he was where he should've been. And that was something he couldn't make Tess understand. He wasn't sure it was something any civilian could truly understand.

In a rare moment of defeat, he headed home. He seldom went there anymore except to sleep.

His neighborhood, also on the west side of the city, was tucked into one of the many enclaves you couldn't see from the main road.

The curving driveway had been positioned to take advantage of the fifty-foot trees on the lot when Cole had bought it. They blocked the house from the street, making it seem like little more than a passing blur of glass, stone and steel. Cole had designed the house himself. He liked sleek, uncluttered lines, but he wasn't into sterile. The walls were painted subtle shades of sage and brown. The floors, rich cherrywood. A massive tumbled marble fireplace took up one wall of the main living area.

Skylights and a bank of two-story windows

at the front of the house allowed light deep inside. The house suited him, but Cole had mortgaged it to put cash into the company. As much as he liked the place, it would be gone if the business didn't recover.

Removing his jacket, he built a fire. His Siamese cats, Harley and Horace, followed him to the kitchen, winding themselves around his legs. He opened some canned food, a treat from their usual dry, and gave them each some attention, even though he knew—typical cats—they barely missed him when he was gone.

Harley hopped up on the counter, and the doorbell rang a moment later. Cole didn't want to be bothered answering it, but he dragged himself out to the hall anyway, Horace at his feet.

"I should've called," Tess said quickly when he opened the door. She looked uncertain.

He opened the door wide. "Come in."

"The house is very you," she said stepping inside, her attention drawn to the vaulted ceilings and the masses of glass.

"Is that good?"

"Yes."

"Have you had dinner?"

She shook her head.

"Raiding my refrigerator isn't even decent sport, but I can offer you a glass of wine."

"You didn't tell me you had pets."

He shrugged. "They like to keep a low profile."

She knelt holding out her hands. Harley, bolder than Horace, ventured near. "What are their names?"

He told her, adding, "Horace is the more intellectual one."

The cats kept a proper distance, which Tess respected, although they followed as she wandered over to the bookcases.

Cole found a bottle of wine and opened it while she read some of his titles.

"You like James Elroy?" she asked, her back to him.

"He's a little grim for some people's taste, but I admire his work. No one writes crime in L.A. like he does."

She mulled through a few more books. "So many technical engineering books. Do they relax you on a quiet Sunday afternoon?"

"Not particularly." He gestured toward the kitchen. "I probably have some chips or crackers stashed away in here."

She turned around. "That's okay."

He brought in the wine, handing her a glass. "Then I'll buy you dinner instead."

"Deal." She sipped her wine, hesitated. "I heard you visited Ron today at the hospital."

"Some grapevine for a big place."

"His fiancée told me. That was a nice thing to do, Cole."

"We just happened to be on the same elevator. It was a natural thing to take him to his room."

"No, I mean talking to him. Whatever you said, his attitude seemed to improve. I don't mean a total turnaround. Just a little better. He's been bleak for so long, you gave Mary hope."

"I was glad to do it. Tess, I don't want to hobble the gift horse, but this is one of the times when I don't think we're on opposite sides. I hate to see what happened to Ron as much as you do."

"Does that mean you'll join my cause?"

He blew out an exasperated breath. "I hate to see any soldier injured—or worse. And I feel guilty as hell seeing people like Ron when I was able to walk away."

"You were wounded."

He snorted. "Nothing by comparison."

"I don't understand this…this *soldier* thing."

Cole's patience returned bit by bit. "I know you don't."

Her expression relaxed marginally. "Oh?"

"Yeah."

Harley meowed.

Distracted, she glanced down at the cat. "You think that means I can pet him now?"

"He'll accept small offers of worship."

She stroked the cat. "You're a beautiful boy."

"He knows. They both do. My family spoiled them rotten while I was gone."

Horace shyly rubbed her leg. "What a sweetie."

"My boys are loving you."

She looked up at him then, with those thick lashes and incredible, color-changing eyes of hers. Eyes capable of shifting everything inside him.

Tess raised her face until her lips were just below his. Every reason to pull away, to not get involved with this man, was a shout that lessened to a benign whisper as his hands threaded through her hair, caressed her neck, stroked her back. Why had his letters fallen into her hands? Wasn't that fate?

Their kiss deepened, and she shuddered. Her breathing became ragged as he explored her neck, nipping the tender flesh beneath her earlobe.

His hands pulled at her clothing. Hers at his.

Air seemed scarce, the space between them even scarcer.

When the cell phone on Cole's belt emitted a harsh, unusual shriek, it sounded like an explosion.

He swore.

It took Tess a moment to recognize what was happening.

"It's the 911 signal from the plant."

She sat up, straightening her clothes. "Of course." She tucked her blouse in. "Do you know what it is?"

"Injury." He read the text. "I'm not sure how serious. They took someone by ambulance to the hospital."

"Then you have to go."

He hesitated. "Hell, Tess."

She stood. "No. You have to see about this person. It's what I'd do." She searched for her shoes, which she'd apparently slipped off. She tried not to appear as rattled as she felt.

"I'll make up for that dinner."

"Uh-huh." And she fled.

Fate.

She wondered if fate had just dialed Cole's cell phone. With a 911 alert no less.

CHAPTER THIRTEEN

TESS COULDN'T CONCENTRATE on her work. Cole had called to let her know his employee's injury wasn't serious, that he would recover without any lasting ill effects. That was a relief, but still, what was she doing, furthering this relationship with Cole? A military man.

Getting little done, she decided to visit her father, who seemed to have come down with something. Her mother had reassured her that there was nothing seriously wrong with him, but Tess decided to check for herself.

Her parents' home was quiet as she let herself in through the back door. The kitchen was tidy. The tea kettle was heating. A single mug with a tea bag sat on the counter.

Tillie, the cat, meowed a greeting, winding around her legs. Tess gave her a perfunctory scratch behind the ear, then went in search of her father. "Dad?"

The den, where he could usually be found, was empty. Tess glanced out the wide windows into the backyard. The house she'd grown up in was more than fifty years old and mature trees towered over the yard, providing a comfortable mix of shade and filtered sunlight. Her father sat outside at the table, his profile to her.

He had aged since David's death. His thick, once black hair was now mostly gray. Sadness had etched deep furrows in his face. And there was a sag in his posture that had never been there before. *Oh, David. He misses you so.*

Tess opened the sliding glass door and the cat scooted out in front of her.

Her father turned, his face brightening. "Tess!"

She smiled, hoping her thoughts didn't show in her face. "Hi, Dad." She kissed his cheek. "It's a great day to be outside."

He glanced back at the jungle gym and wooden playhouse he'd been studying. "You and David used to play out here for hours."

"When it rained, David would put up a pirate flag and declare the playhouse his ship."

Her father smiled. "He always did want to be in charge."

"Probably because he was good at it."

"You are, too," Thomas asserted. "But you're trying to do too much." He touched the newspaper spread out on the tabletop. "And I'm not helping by playing hooky."

"Mom said you have the flu or a virus."

He shook his head. "No, I'm just tired. Needed a little time."

"You've earned it, Dad. I can put in some extra hours, help out Mom more."

"You're already putting in too much time." He sighed. "It wasn't supposed to turn out this way."

Her throat closed. And for a few minutes they let the quiet of the morning settle over them.

"I've been thinking, Dad. About the permanent management positions." She took a deep breath. "What would you think of asking Eric and Joseph to be part of the business?"

Thomas frowned. "They're not Spencers."

"But they *are* family."

"I always thought your children and David's would eventually take over the restaurants."

Tess blinked several times. "But I don't think

David would want you working yourself to exhaustion. And Mother's family was always important to him."

"Would the boys even want to leave the jobs they have now?"

Leaning forward, she took his hand. "I don't know. I'll have to ask them."

Thomas sighed. "I'm getting old, Tess."

"You're just tired, Dad."

"Maybe." He studied her closely. "Is there something you're not telling me, punkin?"

She warmed under the old nickname. "Just remembering when we were last all together." And, even though she should rush back to the restaurant, she sat there with her father. She'd learned the hard way these were the moments she could never reclaim.

IT ONLY TOOK A WEEK for Eric and Joseph to settle with their existing jobs and officially join Spencers management.

By eleven that night the restaurant was mercifully quiet. Quiet enough that Tess was confident about leaving her assistant to close. Outside, the streets were still busy, but Tess was accustomed to the constant hustle.

As she drove toward the intersection, she hesitated. She could make her usual left turn and go to the downtown location, check on everything there. Or she could go in the opposite direction. One that would take her to Cole's office. She didn't even consider that he might be home. He often stayed late at the plant.

A car honked behind her, ending the indecision. Turning right, she entered the freeway on-ramp, merging with the considerable traffic. Not the commuter crawl, but as busy as many cities would be in midmorning except now it was almost midnight.

It didn't take long to reach Harrington Engineering. The lights in the parking lot were on and plenty of cars filled the spaces.

But now that she was here, Tess wasn't sure what to do next. Just as she was reconsidering her out-of-the-way detour, she recognized Mark Cannon at one of the cars. Probably going home, since it was ridiculously late. She opened her door and called out to him.

He opened the lid of his trunk at nearly the same time and turned, obviously startled.

"I don't know if you remember me. I met you here a few weeks ago. Tess Spencer."

"I remember. Kind of late to be stopping by, isn't it?" He put several large padded envelopes in the trunk, then closed the lid.

"I was hoping to pop in on Cole, but I hadn't thought about how I was going to get inside," she explained.

"No problem. We can go through the side entrance."

"It's not locked?"

"Everything's locked, but my pass will get us in." He pointed across the lot. "Cole's car is here, so he should be, too."

"You're working long hours as well," Tess sympathized as they walked to the building.

"It's for a good cause." He slipped his key card into the slot and they listened to the click. Mark pushed the door open and held it for her.

"Thank you."

"Do you want me to try to find Cole for you? It's a bit dark in here with the energy-saving night system on," he asked.

"That's okay, I know the way. I don't want to keep you when it's so late."

"Well, there are quite a few people around. So if you change your mind, just ask anybody." He smiled and then headed across the dim corridor.

With the door closed behind her, the building sounded terribly quiet. Where were all these people, then? Shaking off an annoying shiver, she made her way in the other direction down the hall.

She was prepared to knock on Cole's office door, but it was open. And it only took a moment to see that the room was empty. Disappointed, she wondered if she had somehow missed him in the parking lot.

She ventured into the reception area, but it was empty and dark. Uneasy, she decided to give up her impromptu visit. Guided by the lights from the parking lot, she tried one of the tall, heavy glass doors that led outside.

But it simply made a clicking noise. And not the same one the side door had. This one ended in a buzzing sound. She pushed again. This time the buzzing started immediately.

"Must not be the right exit," she muttered.

She headed back to the side door. At the same instant, an alarm started shrieking. Horrified, she ran back to the door, pulling it toward her, trying to turn off what she'd triggered. The alarm intensified.

Tess backed away from the door, trying to decide what to do. She'd only taken a few steps when the alarm came to a sudden halt. Surprise changed to fright when she thudded into something solid, warm. *Someone* solid. Her heart in her throat, she tried to talk, but her voice came out as a squeak. "Who's there?"

Fingers closed around her arm, and she was turned around.

"Tess?"

She stared into the darkness, picking out Cole's features. "You scared me to death!"

"You nearly gave me a heart attack. You set off alarms all over the building."

"I'm painfully aware of that." She managed a limp smile. "I was trying to surprise you."

"It worked." Some of his humor had obviously returned. "How did you get in?"

"Mark Cannon."

A few seconds passed.

They both burst out laughing.

Tess laughed until she was weak, until she had to lean against Cole for support. And she stayed there until she caught her breath.

She lifted her face, her mouth seeking his. She didn't know if it was the intimate darkness, the dregs of adrenaline or just the heat he stirred in her. But she was bold, reckless as their mouths met, as his hands pulled her close, then slipped beneath her blouse to glide against her back.

And just as suddenly he was pulling away. "Oh, hell."

"What?"

"Security will be here any second. They're going from exit to exit. I took this one because I was closest." He straightened her blouse, then switched on the lights.

She smoothed her hair as she heard the sound of footsteps approaching.

"False alarm," Cole told the man who arrived. "Ms. Spencer accidentally triggered it."

"Yes, sir. I'll relay the all clear."

After the security man retreated, Tess was more than a little abashed. "You're still working."

"Not anymore."

"I just planned to stop by for a minute. I know it's late and I still have to go downtown."

"Can't you skip it?"

"I feel like an idiot, setting off alarms and everything. I only came by to tell you about Eric and Joseph. They're going to come to work at the restaurants."

"That's great." He studied her. "Isn't it?"

"Of course. It's just a big change."

"Something had to change," he said.

"I know." She closed her eyes for a moment realizing she sounded like a truculent child. Opening them, she swallowed. "I do, you know. But I don't have to like it right off, do I?"

"No. Not today." He hugged her. "Not to-day."

CHAPTER FOURTEEN

COLE FOUND Allen at the airport hangar, in his office. He tossed a new security badge on his desk. "Your old one's obsolete."

Allen leaned back in his chair, propping his feet on a well-used leather trunk. "I don't suppose you've figured out who stole your designs."

"No. I upgraded the security system, nothing."

Allen studied him over the rim of his coffee mug. "Tess work out the restaurant problem?"

Cole took a sip of the thick coffee. "She brought in two of her cousins. They're naturals apparently."

"So, what's the problem?"

"She's still spending too much time working. And now she's volunteering at the hospital when she has a spare hour."

Allen couldn't completely hide his smile. "Feeling neglected, are we?"

"Don't be a sap."

"You *are!*" Surprise gave way to amusement.

"She's having a hard time figuring things out since her brother was killed."

Allen's amusement gave way to sympathy. "She still thinks his death was a waste?"

"Yes."

"Can't you help her with that?"

"We talk about it, but she's got to decide what she believes. And I think that's the real reason she keeps her schedule so crowded. Then she doesn't have to question whether she can cope with me."

"Maybe by meeting vets at the hospital she'll get a sense of why you and her brother had to serve."

Cole wasn't so sure. "Or just the opposite. Seeing the wounded, hearing what they've gone through. It's a lot for anyone, but Tess takes it all to heart." Too much to heart.

Allen knew him so well he didn't prod, didn't question his long silence.

Cole took a deep swallow of coffee. "I haven't got one thing in my life straight."

Allen swung his feet down from the trunk. "That's pretty harsh. I know you. If this was only about the company, you wouldn't have left the plant long enough to come out here. But no computer program can figure out Tess, can it?"

Allen had him there. And he was right about the business. As much as it mattered to him, he was more concerned about Tess.

Allen picked up the coffeepot and refilled both mugs. "Don't look so gutted. It had to happen eventually. Even to you, my friend."

TESS HADN'T INTENDED to become so involved in the patients' lives at the spinal injury unit, but it was difficult to stay detached. Many of those she saw on a regular basis had had more surgeries than they could keep track of. And they were there on an extended basis. Most had no idea when they'd be released.

The toughest cases were the people who'd never walk again. But there was camaraderie among them. Similar to what they shared in combat.

"Come on, Travis, move those legs," Johnson goaded him.

"I'm dancing now," Travis retorted.

Both had limited movement, but it didn't stop their determination.

"Did you know each other in the Army?" Tess asked.

"Nah, met here," Travis replied.

"I'm in the Corps," Johnson told her.

"And won't ever let you forget it," Travis added.

"Oh. So you weren't even in the same branch of the service?"

"No, ma'am."

"Just Tess. I thought since you're friends you must have known each other before."

"We're just stuck in the same hospital," Travis told her.

"Speak for yourself," Johnson said.

"They aren't letting us go back to our units," Travis explained.

Tess stared at them. "You'd want to return?"

Johnson snorted. "Damn straight."

"Sure," Travis said barely a second later.

"But you were hurt so badly." Tess hesitated. "What if…"

Johnson pulled up on his exercise bar. "Ma'am, with all due respect, it's not my job to die for my country. It's my job to make the other poor bastard die for his."

Tess gaped at him.

"What he says," Travis added. "We're not a bunch of hotheaded idiots. We believe in what we're doing."

Tess refilled the water pitcher. "What makes you believe in it?"

Travis met her gaze. "Well, ma'am, you walk up to a bunch of little kids who didn't have nothing for years. And we've been able to build them schools. Schools girls can go to. Little girls like mine. And when they see us, their faces light up. They're happy to see Americans. They don't see us as the bad guys. People go on about how we're ruining the future over there. We're building a future, 'cause those kids *are* the future. They watch us. They see what we're doing. And, yeah, they see us get blown up by some of their own idiots, too. And they remember that, too."

Tess bit her lip. Had David helped make an impact, as this soldier had said? Had his death not been a waste? "You really think so?"

"Yes, ma'am, I do."

"How does your wife cope with you serving in the Army?"

"She's a strong woman who believes I'm doing the right thing for our country, for our family."

Tess swallowed. That was the flaw in his reasoning. She didn't have the strength.

"Can I get you anything else?"

He glanced at her Families of the Fallen pin. Then he smiled, a surprisingly sweet smile on his tough face. "No, ma'am. Just keep supporting our guys over there. That's all we need."

THE DE VILLARD family property in Magnolia, about forty miles outside of Houston, consisted of a two-story Norman stone farmhouse, sturdy barn, stable and acres of green pastures.

Tess's grandparents now lived in Houston, close enough for the family to check on them often, but they hadn't sold the farm. Neighbors leased the pastureland for grazing. Family members cared for their own horses and took turns maintaining the house.

Cole whistled. "The place is so pristine, it's like it was frozen in time."

"The farm looks just like it did when my grandparents lived here. They love this place."

"Sounds like you do, too."

The breeze tousled her hair. "There were so many good times here. And back then, the world seemed so much safer, saner...."

Cole took her hand, not saying anything as they walked to the barn. Tess guided him to a pair of adjoining stalls.

She stopped at the first one. A mare thrust her head forward and Tess stroked her face. "This is Shortcake. She's mine."

"Beautiful quarter horse."

Tess fished in her pocket for a carrot, fed it to Shortcake and moved to the next stall.

An elegant palomino greeted Tess like an old friend, and she gave him a carrot as well. "And this is Dancer."

"David's horse."

Nodding, she stroked the horse's neck. "I haven't been out here for months."

"Who's been riding them?"

"My younger cousins. They like earning extra money taking care of them."

"You miss your horse."

"Uh-huh. Tack's over there." She pointed.

It didn't take long to saddle up. Since the horses were ridden regularly, they weren't difficult to control. On command, Shortcake and Dancer eased into a gallop across the fields.

Tess realized just how much she'd missed this. Coming back to the farm, to her roots.

They kept up the fast pace until they approached the back acreage, thick with oak trees. Near the pond, they dismounted and led the horses to the grassy bank.

"Dancer loved the workout." Tess picked a blade of grass. "Sundays here used to be so great."

Cole studied her face. "You make it sound as though that's all in the past."

"We stopped having the lunches after…"

"I don't mean the Sunday lunches. I mean the happy times."

She shredded the blade of grass. "Much as I might want to, I can't turn back the calendar."

"Tess, you don't have to choose between the past and the future. David's gone, but you aren't."

She sucked in her breath at the direct words. "You don't know what you're talking about."

"I dealt with life and death on a daily basis. You *choose* how to deal with what you get, Tess. You can throw away today and tomorrow. But before you do, ask yourself, what would David have done with that same time?"

It wasn't a fair question. Unfair, unasked for. But the truth in his words hit her. Hard.

Cole smoothed her hair. "Tess, I know there are always going to be times when you miss your brother. But don't you think he deserves to be remembered with happiness, as well?"

"Of course I do!"

"What would have made David happy? You said Sundays here were great. For him, too?"

"Yes."

"Why not plan a big Sunday lunch at the farmhouse? Like you used to. Something you would've done when David was alive. Do you think the family would be up for it?"

Her throat tightened, she missed her twin so much. "Probably."

"I hear some of your relatives even cook."

"Yeah."

"Would it help your parents?"

"I think maybe it would. My mom especially." Tess tossed the shredded grass aside. "You're right. I'd like to see if Ron could get a pass…you know, to join us for lunch. And his fiancée, too."

"Sounds like something your brother would've liked." He took her hand. "Something he would definitely have approved of."

CHAPTER FIFTEEN

COLE STOOD BACK and watched the De Villard family in action. Otherwise, he was pretty sure he'd have gotten trampled. As they planned the first lunch, all the aunts, uncles and cousins agreed they wanted to start up the tradition again and would take turns hosting. And even though the farmhouse was kept clean, they pitched in with lemon oil, dusters and the like until every surface gleamed, every window sparkled for the renewal of their beloved custom.

The men set up tables on the lawn beneath the shade of the old oak trees. The women spread tablecloths, settled dishes in place, then added nosegays of daisies and violets. The kitchen was filled with the aroma of newly baked bread, sweet potatoes and roasted corn.

Outside, a huge turkey and ham roasted on

separate rotisseries of the stone barbecue while the prime rib took center rack.

One table was stacked with desserts. Cole stopped looking after he'd spotted the apple pie and New York style cheesecake.

The maiden Spencer aunts arrived with Tess's parents. Eric had been given command of the landmark restaurant for the day, enabling them to attend. He and Joseph had outstripped Tess's best expectations.

Judith's brothers, sisters and parents surrounded her, obviously thrilled to be together again at their family home. Cole didn't want to interrupt.

Until he saw Sandy struggling with a large platter. "Looks like you could use some help." He slipped his hands beneath the dish.

"Thanks. It didn't seem that heavy in the kitchen."

He laid the plate on the table. "More to bring out, I suppose."

"Yes. But we can take a quick break. Right now there are so many bodies in the kitchen it's a wonder the house doesn't tip over." She fanned her face. "It's great being out here again."

"I understand it's been a while."

"It didn't seem right to just go on with our Sunday celebrations as though nothing had happened. And then, well, it's been months. But Tess, Aunt Judith and Uncle Thomas…well, you know."

"They weren't ready to move on, get back into the old routine."

"Exactly." Sandy plunged her hands in her pockets. "I don't suppose I should say this, but you seem very good for our Tess. She smiles more…well, more than she has since David died. And a few months ago, she never would have participated in this, much less have been the one to get them started again. I'm glad you've come into her life."

Touched, Cole wasn't sure how to reply.

"Don't worry. I don't expect an answer." She grinned. "I'm glad I'm not a man. I'd be dying to blab all the time. Now I'd better battle my way back into the kitchen."

"I can help."

"It's all right. Besides, I think I see Tess heading toward the barbecue." With another grin, Sandy went back to the house.

Tess was basting the meat when he reached her. Without breaking stride, she greeted him. "Hey, you."

"You know how to throw a party, lady."

"Helps to have an instant guest list of people who like being together."

"Thanks for adding me to the list."

Her expression softened, even though her eyes held a troubled look he recognized. One that said she was thinking their alliance was unwise. Unfortunately, it was a look he saw more and more often. As she pulled farther and farther away.

He was about to say something he'd probably regret when he spotted Mary pushing Ron's wheelchair up the sidewalk. So she had invited them.

"Ron. Glad you made it," Cole said, shaking his hand. "And this must be Mary."

"We wouldn't have missed it," Mary replied.

"I hope I won't be in the way," Ron muttered.

"Of course not," Tess reassured him, as she took the salad Mary offered her. "Let me just put this out."

As Tess left Cole to make introductions, he indicated the old farmhouse. "Tess's grandparents built it when they settled here," he explained.

Ron nodded.

"It's lovely," Mary agreed. "It was kind of Tess to invite us."

Yes, but that was Tess.

"There are two other patients in the van," Mary added. "I think the driver'll need help with a wheelchair."

"I'll do that. See you guys in a while."

The two patients were older vets from the Second World War who lived in the nursing home unit of the hospital and had no family. Cole grinned, thinking they might just have inherited a larger one than they ever wanted. Glancing up he caught sight of Rachel and Jim and his smile faded.

He watched as Rachel introduced Jim to various family members. Jim seemed happy, relaxed. Something he hadn't been at work since Cole spoke to him about Rachel.

Something they would have to remedy.

In a short while, the food laid out on the tables, everyone came together to eat. Judith's oldest brother stood to make a toast. "To Tess, for bringing us all back together. To Judith and Thomas, who we love. And to David, who we will never forget."

Tess's lips trembled as she accepted the toast,

then laughed as she clinked numerous glasses with her own. Everyone seemed to talk at once, at least a dozen conversations overlapping, dovetailing.

As Cole had expected, the vets from the nursing home were made to feel included. Tess's aunts and uncles, especially the older ones, drew them in like old friends.

Jim spent a great deal of time talking to Ron. Cole couldn't decide if it was an accident of seating or Tess's plan that they were beside each other. But he didn't question that or anything else.

This was Tess's special day.

So after the meal was eaten, while the kids wandered off to games, and some of the adults lingered over coffee, Cole took her hand and they walked the path beneath the century-old magnolia trees. But he saved his questions. Hoping he had plenty of time to ask them.

ONLY COLE and Nate were at the 6:00 a.m. meeting the following Tuesday.

"*Hidden* cameras in the design department?" Nate asked.

"The designers aren't going to be able to work

up to their creative capacity if they can see them."

"What does Jim think about this?"

Cole swivelled his chair away from Nate, staring out at the dawn-tinged sky.

"Cole?"

"He's not to know about the cameras."

Silence pulsed between them. Jim and Nate were also friends.

Nate finally sighed. "It's a damned business."

"Agreed."

"I'll install them tonight after they're all gone. Do you want me to monitor them myself?"

"Yes. I don't want anyone else, even security, to know about them."

"I hope to hell you're wrong about him."

Cole didn't turn. "Me, too."

"WHO'S DOING BETTER?" Thomas asked several weeks later. "Eric or Joseph?"

Tess hesitated. "You know them, Dad. They're strong-willed, smart, resourceful."

Surprisingly he smiled. "Just like your Spencer side."

Relieved, she hugged him.

Thomas continued smiling. "Do you think one of them is good enough to run the Galleria?"

She drew back.

"Your mother and I can't run the landmark location forever."

Shocked, she stared at him. She hadn't known her father was thinking that far ahead. "Is there something you want to tell me?"

"If the boys become good managers, then we have options."

Boys. They were both close to her age. She was relieved her father was accepting their ability. But his acknowledgment of aging was frightening.

"And we have years to decide," she murmured. Suddenly, her parents' fragility gripped her. And she was as terrified as she'd been when she was seven years old and had lost her mother's hand in the crowded downtown Woolworth's.

"Don't worry about it now." He patted her hand. "And, Tess, I'm glad you started up the Sunday lunches at the farm again. We needed that, all of us."

Cole's idea.

"I like that young man of yours," he added.

"He's not *my* young man."

Thomas smiled. "Oh, I think so. A man doesn't look at a woman the way Cole does unless his heart is involved."

Tess's breath caught, and she sputtered. "Dad, you must have been seeing what you wanted to see."

"No. I'm not in any hurry to relinquish my little girl."

She hugged him again, hanging on to his familiar warmth. For strength. Because *her* heart was certainly involved. She'd waited too long.

COLE STUDIED the hidden camera security reports for the dozenth time. No irregularities. Nate hadn't found anything on the tapes to report.

Not that Cole wanted him to. He didn't want his friend to prove to be a thief. And Jim had been on his mind. For weeks they'd politely avoided each other.

And it was eating into him.

Cole checked his watch. It was late. The designers should all be gone. But Jim was usually the last one to leave.

The lights were still on in the creative department. Cole used his badge to get through the main entrance. The series of clicks alerted Jim, who looked surprised and not particularly pleased.

"I wasn't sure you'd still be here."

"Just finishing up." Jim snapped off the printer.

"You have a minute?"

"Guess so."

"I don't like what's between us, Jim."

"I didn't put it there."

Cole considered their years of friendship. "I was out of line. It's none of my business who you date."

Jim was silent for so long, Cole wondered if he'd accept the apology.

"I don't understand what you've got against Rachel. Sure, she comes across as edgy, but that's not what she's all about."

"Like Tess. It's not all Spencers and war protests."

"I hadn't heard about the war protests," Jim reflected. "Is that why Tess invited Ron to the farm? I really liked talking to him." Jim scratched his head. "Damn shame about his sight. Brilliant software engineer. Did he tell you he designed the entire line of Mecca Litz software before he was deployed? And now the guy figures he'll never design again. He must have a head full of ideas."

"It's just getting them from his head to production," Cole muttered.

"What?"

"Thinking out loud. How much do you know about Braille software?"

"A little. I did some checking after I talked with Ron and—" Jim's cell phone rang, a crazy tune that was typical Jim. From the way he answered, Cole suspected Rachel was the caller. He mouthed good-night.

And hoped Jim had judged Rachel correctly. Back in his office he phoned Tess, but she said she couldn't see him. Again. She was still pulling away and he didn't know how to stop her.

SURPRISE HAD ALWAYS been a good tactic. A week later Cole decided to use it. He knew by now that, midweek at her restaurant, Joseph would have things under control.

He also knew that calling ahead to make sure was a good idea. It was an even better idea to enlist some male support. And Joseph was willing.

So when Cole arrived at the Galleria restaurant, Tess had little choice, unless she wanted to make a scene, other than to go with him.

"You should have called."

"So you could tell me how busy you are?"

"I have been busy," she insisted.

He didn't want to push, fairly certain what he'd hear if he did. "Then you need to relax."

"I have things to do at the restaurant."

"Joseph assured me he could handle things tonight."

From her expression, Cole guessed Joseph was going to hear plenty about his mutiny. "I have three restaurants to worry about."

"Not tonight. Please?"

"Cole…" She sighed, then glanced out the window. "Okay."

The route was familiar. And Tess wasn't surprised when he took the airport exit. There were a lot of thoughts to sort out. A lot of words they needed to say. That she needed to say.

He pulled in front of the hangar, this time parking near a small airstrip off to the side. An old airplane, lights on, engine running, sat on the airstrip.

"There's our ride."

"I don't carry my passport," she replied weakly.

"It's not big enough to go to Paris."

Dazed, she let him propel her out of the car and up the stairs into the small plane. Allen greeted her, added her ID to his itinerary, already prepared. It didn't take long to strap in, then they were navigating down the shorter runway for small planes.

The vintage plane bumped its way through the darkness, lifting off smoothly, then rose into the sky. There was something magical about taking off in the night, all the lights of the city spread out below.

"It's like a fairyland," she murmured, watching out the window. "It doesn't seem real."

It took a few minutes for the noise to quiet somewhat, so Tess studied the interior of the plane. She realized it must date back to the Second World War. Leather seats, wooden insets. How ironic. If she'd met Cole then… Maybe she could've held on to her patriotic ideals…and Cole.

"I've missed you."

She swallowed. "Cole—"

"Don't tell me something I'm not ready to hear."

"I tell myself I should just enjoy today, but I can't. I know myself too well."

He threaded his fingers through hers. "I liked the part about enjoying today."

She dropped her chin, feeling the start of tears. "Can you give up the Reserves?"

"Tess…"

Allen dipped the plane in the clouds, taking them over the great expanse of the city. And she let the tears fall.

THE FOLLOWING DAY, restless, Cole drove to the veterans' hospital. But Ron was asleep, exhausted, Mary had told him. So he left without seeing him.

He'd gotten to know the younger soldier fairly well since they'd met. He was researching some options in hopes that Ron could continue working in design, but until he knew for sure, he didn't want to raise his hopes.

He hadn't broken through the shell Ron had constructed. Not that Cole blamed him. At twenty-five years old, his dreams were smashed.

Cole wasn't going to give up on him. Therapists worked with Ron to teach him how to live as a blind man in a sighted world, but Ron had lost his belief.

Yet sometimes even a sighted man could be blind. Cole should have anticipated Tess's reaction to his being in the Reserves, that she'd start to pull away bit by bit. She'd made it clear she didn't believe in fighting another country's war, that she thought David's death was futile.

But he'd hoped she would change her mind. Stupid, he supposed. How could he tell her, that despite the complicated realities of this war, a soldier didn't stay in or get out for just one cause. The long deployment had done more than endanger his company. It had bonded him with the men and women of his unit. And he couldn't let them down by walking away.

But he couldn't let Tess walk away either. And she was trying hard.

CHAPTER SIXTEEN

THE FAMILY REUNIONS had come into their own again at the farmhouse. Revived by the renewed activity every Sunday. Even the air seemed fresher, welcoming.

In turn, the De Villards welcomed all the ambulatory long-term patients Tess invited from the hospital—those able to get day passes. And especially those she knew didn't get visitors. Plenty she wanted to invite were too badly injured and couldn't leave their beds. "I wish I had a way to bring Johnson and Travis."

"You can't save the entire world," Cole reminded her.

"Isn't that what you're trying to do?" She picked at the food on her plate. "I'm not the one in the Reserves."

"I could point out how happy you've made the two older gentlemen your family adopted."

Tess relaxed marginally as they watched the veterans, who were now regulars.

"And Ron," Cole continued. "Look how comfortable he is talking software with Jim. A month ago you couldn't get two words out of him, even with his girl."

"He and Mary are sweet," Tess said.

And Cole had to admit that even Rachel and Jim seemed good together. It was difficult to believe. But she did actually appear softer with him.

"Tess, you remember the laptop you returned to me?"

She looked at him, inquisitive. "Very well."

"You remember telling me you got it at the auction?"

"Yes."

"Well, it wasn't on the consignment."

"I know."

"You do?"

She nodded. "I bought a desk and a file cabinet. Well, actually Sandy bought the desk. I wanted the file cabinet. And when the porter started to load it in the back of the Lexus we heard the laptop rattling around. I told him we hadn't paid for a computer, but he said those were the rules of the auction, that the seller knows anything left in the furniture goes with the consignment. I would have explained that, but you got so—"

"Pissed."

"But when I read the letters, well…you know the rest."

Which meant Rachel had absolutely nothing to do with the theft of his designs, or the threat to his company. Ashamed of his suspicions, Cole wondered what else he'd gotten wrong.

"Thanks for letting me come today, Tess."

She glanced down at the table, hating what she had to say. "I just don't see much point, Cole. The longer I keep seeing you…the harder it is to say…goodbye."

He put down his fork. "Isn't there some room for compromise?"

"What kind of compromise?" Her stomach roiled. "If you're deployed, you don't go?"

"Tess, you know that can't happen."

"What kind of compromise is there?" She wanted one. Any kind.

"So that's it?"

She traced the tiny scars on his hand, not willing to let him go yet. "You know it's not what I want."

"It's what you're saying."

"Can you promise you won't get hurt?"

"Tess—"

"Or die?"

"No, I can't."

The lump in her throat was so big she had to concentrate so she could swallow. She stared even harder at the lines in his hand as they blurred. "You could just not reenlist. You've done your duty."

"You could have faith in me, Tess. You don't have to support the reasons I want to be in the Reserves, just support me."

She lifted her gaze, not caring when the first tear fell. "See? It's not going to change." She took a shaky breath. "And you're going to break my heart."

"Tess, this isn't what I want."

She brushed away the tears. "Me neither."

"Why don't we talk somewhere away from here?"

"And say what? What haven't we already said, Cole?"

"Can I take you home?"

She shook her head. "I'll ride with Kate or Sandy."

"Tess…"

"Please, Cole. Don't make it worse." She couldn't watch as he walked away. And for the longest time she sat alone at the table. It hadn't worked, she realized. Her heart wasn't immune.

THE BREEZE STIRRED just enough to rustle the leaves in the tall oaks and tease the scent from the roses and freshly cut grass. But Tess didn't notice any of it.

She barely noticed when Sandy approached her table. "I saw Cole leave. What's going on?"

"Just the same thing."

"Tess, not about the Reserves again."

"Yes."

"You didn't let him leave because of that?"

Tess wiped her eyes. "I asked him to."

"You didn't!"

"Would you stop? Please?"

"Tess, I don't understand." She sighed. "I guess you have your reasons. Inexplicable as they are. Anyway, don't sit over here by yourself. Come on."

Kate and Rachel greeted Tess when she joined them at their table. Jim had left to help Ron into the van.

"When will Cole be back?" Rachel asked.

Tess fiddled with her glass of iced tea. "He won't."

"Does he have to work?" Kate asked.

"His company takes most of his time," Tess said, evading the question.

Sandy rolled her eyes.

Tess shot her a warning glare.

Rachel's radar picked it up immediately. "Okay. What's wrong between Cinderella and Prince Charming?"

Tess wanted to choke Sandy. This, this… thing between her and Cole was too raw to talk about. "Rachel, my life is not a prospectus for you to dissect."

"Touchy, aren't we? You know I'm on your side, so give."

Rachel would nag until she got what she wanted. And it was concern that motivated her, so Tess relented. "Cole is in the Reserves."

"You mean he has to go for training?" Kate asked.

"No. Just that he's *in* the Reserves. So we're not seeing each other anymore."

Rachel, for once, looked stumped. "And that's a problem, why?"

Kate jogged Tess's shoulder. "Isn't it obvious, Rach? She's scared he could be deployed again and hurt." Despite her sometimes naive take on life, Kate's intuitiveness usually hit a home run.

Rachel drew her eyebrows together. "You're not dumping a great guy like Cole because of that, are you?"

"How can I open myself up to that kind of pain?"

Rachel draped one arm over Tess's shoulders. "You can't ditch a wonderful relationship because we lost David."

"David would've blasted you one," Sandy agreed.

"Tessie." Rachel shook her head. "You can't avoid pain by avoiding men like Cole."

"Like Cole?"

"Someone willing to go when his country calls. Do you want to find someone who would say no?"

Tears clogged her throat, choking all her arguments.

Kate patted her arm. "We know it hurts."

Sandy's eyes misted. "We just don't want you to throw away the best thing that's happened to you in a long time."

Tess looked at her three cousins. "I know you're trying to help. But there's no easy fix." Not for her. Not with Cole.

THREE WEEKS LATER it was time to celebrate. Even to brag. The preliminary designs were complete. The mood at Harrington was giddy, nearly smug.

"We can start test runs later tonight," Mark was saying.

"Not a minute too soon. Get the final designs over to Mason ASAP." Cole wanted to tie the deal down. "Nate, we're in good order?"

"I'll call in extra security shifts. Keep them in place until we deliver the sealed bid."

"Right. Jim, anything you need?"

The design manager smiled broadly. "Steaks. Two inches thick. As soon as we get the bid. 'Cause we're going to get it."

Cole took a deep breath. "This is it, men."

There was one more stop he needed to make. One for Tess, even if she wouldn't know about it.

THE HOSPITAL HALLS were no longer over-crowded as they were during the middle of the day. It was eight o'clock in the evening. Still an hour before they chased visitors away.

Ron's room was quiet.

"I'm not asleep."

"Good." Cole pulled up a chair. "You feel like talking?"

Ron hesitated. "I guess."

Cole glanced over at the empty bed in the other half of the room. "No roommate?"

"He left this morning."

Cole cleared his throat. "Will you be ready to go home soon, too?"

"For all that's worth."

Cole heard the defeat in the other man's voice. "Last time I heard, Tess told me you'd about recovered from most of your injuries."

"Yeah."

But not the one that meant the most. "It won't be the same life…but it's life."

"Hell, that's not it," Ron snapped.

"What is it?"

"Are you a therapist now, too?"

"No, just a guy who's felt the fear," Cole admitted. "And the second-guessing."

"But you're not a coward like me. Is that what you're saying?"

"It doesn't seem that way to me."

Ron sighed, a heavy sound in the aftermath of his short outburst. "I knew what the costs were when I enlisted."

"You paid a pretty high price."

"Not as high as some."

Cole tried to figure him out. If his bitterness wasn't because he was blind... "Do you think you should have died?"

Ron's head jerked up, a useless, ingrained habit for a man who couldn't see. "Hell, no. I'm no fool. But I should be handling this better."

"One of my guys lost both legs. Doesn't get worse than that. Except that it did when he got home and found his wife living with another man."

"Hell."

"I've met Mary. She's crazy about you. I don't think you can do anything to run her off."

Ron lifted one hand, then dropped it back on his lap. "She's something."

"I've got a proposition for you."

"Me?"

"Would you join my design team?"

"I don't need your pity."

"It's not. I've got a chance at turning my company around. I need top-notch software designers."

Ron shook his head and started to speak, but Cole cut him off.

"Braille software and a voice module would make it feasible. Models can be built in 3-D out of clay like the ones auto designers use. Or we can manufacture specialized building parts out of flexible plastic right there in the plant."

"I don't know if I can do it," Ron muttered.

"Because you were sighted, you understand spatial relationships. So you'll be able to see the designs, well…you know like Beethoven heard the music. Ron, I almost lost the company. It was damn close. Now that I've got another chance, let me give you one, too. With the work you've done on the Mecca Litz software…well, I know that's the kind of genius I'd be lucky to have. Please think about it." He stood. "Good night."

Ron angled his head, following the sound of Cole's footsteps. Before he left, though, Cole saw hope in his eyes.

HARRINGTON'S preliminary new designs were locked tightly in the high-tech safe. The safe was only one small part of Cole's new security measures. The whole place was shut down tighter than a safety cap on a medicine bottle.

Everyone came and went with a heightened awareness, tension.

Funny thing about security. The more places shut down, the more the leaks could spring. Same with technology. The more it advanced, the cleverer the thieves.

More clever than Cole Harrington by a long shot.

Slipping the thumb-sized flash point disk into a pocket was easy. Short of body searches, Cole would never know if someone walked out with the designs.

Easy as stealing candy from a baby.

CHAPTER SEVENTEEN

COLE STARED at the letter from Mason Industries in disbelief. He had lost the bid. NuDesign had won, based on its innovative proposal.

It wasn't as though he believed no one could compete with him, but his last discussion with Andrew Elderson at Mason had been all but conclusive. Based on the preliminary designs, Elderson believed Harrington was far ahead of the competitors. In fact, Elderson said nothing else he'd seen had even been close.

Turning to his computer, Cole navigated through the networked channels until he found the proposal. Everything looked intact. Nothing had been changed, at least nothing that was indicated on the computer. Then what had happened? Maybe something in the actual package.

Not wasting a second, Cole drove to Mason

Industries. This was something he had to see, to convince himself there hadn't been a mistake.

Elderson admitted him without hesitation, his expression regretful. "I'm sorry, Cole. But I had to go with the best designs."

"Can I look at our package? To make sure everything's there."

Elderson shrugged. "I don't think it will do any good, but you're welcome to look." He rummaged in a desk drawer. "Here you go."

Cole opened the folder, flipping past the correspondence and documentation, going straight to the designs. He studied one. Puzzled, he looked at the next and the next. "These aren't our current designs."

Elderson looked baffled. "What do you mean?"

"Just what I said. Can I look at the ones that won the bid?"

The other man hesitated. "I suppose so. The decision's already been made." He dug into a drawer for the winning folder, then passed it across to Cole.

He opened the file, again going straight for the heart of the matter. "These, *these* are my designs."

Elderson frowned. "No. They belong to NuDesign."

"I don't care what the label says, these are my designs, every last one of them."

"Maybe they seem familiar—"

"Damn right. They're identical copies."

Elderson stared at him.

"Sorry, Andrew. I don't know how NuDesign got these, but I'm going to find out."

"You realize my hands are tied, Cole."

"I understand. But I won't let this just pass."

Elderson sighed. "No, I don't expect you will. But I have a product to manufacture that can't wait. I have to go ahead with these designs."

TESS LISTENED to Ron's fiancée, who couldn't stop talking about Cole.

"He's such a fine man, not even knowing Ron, yet committing so much time to spend with him. And Ron seems more comfortable with him than his old friends. I can see why. Cole doesn't place any expectations on him, so Ron doesn't put up his usual defenses. And Cole knows how it is to have gone to combat. It seems to give them a common bond."

The bond Tess couldn't bear. "I'm glad."

Mary hesitated. "Did I say something wrong?"

"Of course not. You're right. They share a unique experience."

Mary smiled shyly and held up her left hand. "Ron says we're going to get married after all."

"That's wonderful."

"I was beginning to think that no matter how stubborn I was Ron wouldn't change his mind, but whatever Cole said, well, it worked. You're lucky to have a man like him. We both are."

Tess tried not to let the strain show in her smile. "Yes, lucky."

"Will you tell Cole how grateful I am, how grateful we both are?"

"Well, I—"

"Can you believe Cole offered him a job?"

Tess swallowed hard.

"I guess he did all this research and found out that Ron can still design with Braille software. It's going to be so great."

More than simply generous.

"Anyway, I'd really appreciate it if you could talk to him for us. I've tried to call him, but I hate to leave a message. You know, it doesn't seem very personal, especially for something that's going to change our lives."

"I'm sure you could—"

"It's kind of weird calling out there. All I get is voice mail, not even the receptionist. Shouldn't the receptionist answer?"

"Did you call between eight and five?"

"Over and over again. So, could you tell Cole, please?"

Why wasn't Marcia answering? Or someone else if she wasn't there?

BEREFT OF EVEN A SLICE of moonlight, the sky looked ominous. The darkness outside matched Cole's mood. Even though his office blazed with light. He needed it to keep the shadows away.

Deceit, betrayal.

When it was only a suspicion, the thought had angered him. Presented as fact it sickened him.

There was no other explanation.

Someone had not only stolen his designs and presented them as their own. They'd arranged to sabotage his proposal, sealing the fate of the bid.

A lot of hands had touched that final folder.

And because he'd hired based on equality and past relationships, the betrayal was personal.

He stood staring out the window.

Battle instincts made him turn almost before he heard the soft footfalls. Tess stood within arm's reach.

"Cole? What's wrong?"

When he didn't speak immediately, she closed the space between them, lifting her hand to stroke his cheek. "Cole? No one's at reception. I guess because it's so late? I walked right in. Cole?"

Putting his arms around her, Cole held on tightly.

She didn't pull away, sensing his need.

Finally, even though Tess hadn't protested, he released her. She slipped her hand into his.

"Tell me," she said simply.

He recounted the theft.

"Oh, Cole. I'm so sorry. Is it possible it could be a mix-up?"

He shook his head. "It was deliberate."

"Could the other company have switched something with the courier service?"

"We didn't use a courier. Jim took the proposal over in person." As he spoke, the impact of the statement hit him.

"Jim? *Rachel's* Jim?"

"It can't be him. He's been my friend for years."

"Who else had the proposal?"

"Dan Nelson. He put the financials together. Mark Cannon was in charge of the insurance binders. And Marcia. She does my correspondence."

He saw a shadow cross her face.

"What is it, Tess?"

"You remember the night I set off the alarm?"

"Vividly."

She twisted her hands. "This might not be anything, but I ran into Mark in the parking lot. He…he was putting large envelopes in his trunk."

"No way. Not Mark. We worked together for years before I went out on my own. I trusted him enough to leave him in charge of the company while I was deployed." He paused, thinking of the designs he'd been told were scrapped during his absence. "And no one would've been in a better position to divert the proposal." The bitterness of that possibility hit home.

Tess put her slim arm around his waist. "It's a personal betrayal, I know. But you can't blame yourself for trusting people. I'd bet not one of the vets you hired is involved."

"Has something like this ever happened at Spencers?"

"No. I'm just sorry this happened to a good man like you."

"Me, good? Remember I'm military."

Her heart ached for him. "We need to find out who's behind this sabotage."

"We?"

"If you want me to help, that is."

SHE'D COME to Cole's office on Mary and Ron's behalf. But the only person Tess could think of was Cole. And whoever had betrayed him so viciously. What he needed now though wasn't a plan of retaliation.

"I came here in such a rush, I didn't stop to walk the dogs."

"Oh."

"Would you like to join us?"

She tried to gauge the reaction in his eyes. It was something measured, something she'd not seen there before.

"I'd like that."

Tess noticed that Cole didn't seem particularly concerned about security. The reception area was still unmanned. But then there wasn't anything left to steal that mattered.

Cole was quiet as they drove through the darkened streets to her town house. It didn't take long to collect the pets and walk to the nearby park.

Tess lifted her face to the sky. "Can you smell it? There's rain coming."

The wind was picking up, tugging at tree branches, playing with the fallen leaves. Molly and Hector leaned into the increasing currents and Cole carried Scat, the stray she'd adopted. Despite the distraction of the animals, Cole kept her hand tucked in his free one.

Thunder rumbled, so they didn't go far before circling back toward the house. They were still almost a block away when the torrent began. Like upturned buckets of water the rain seemed to pour in a solid sheet. Cole gripped Scat and they all ran.

By the time they reached Tess's building, Scat was screeching at full throttle and they were all soaked. The dogs shook themselves in the hallway. Scat just dug his claws deeper into Cole's arm.

Tess quickly opened the door, and the cat

leaped down and ran to hide. "I'm sorry, Cole. I shouldn't have taken him along. I wasn't thinking."

"He didn't do much damage."

His arm was striped with red scratches. None too deep, but still obviously painful. "Let's get some iodine on those." She led the way into the bedroom, intending to get the first aid kit from the adjoining bathroom.

Cole caught her hand.

She scarcely felt the motion as she turned, coming face-to-face with him, body to body.

Suddenly, frantically aware of the wet clothes that separated them, she fought with the buttons on his shirt. His hands were a bare second behind as he pulled off her shirt. They tugged and tore at buttons, waistbands, anything that got in the way.

Falling on the bed, the press of damp flesh was more illuminating than the flash of lightning that lit the room, then vanished. They slid together, hot despite the cold damp.

Tess felt the nip of air on her bared breasts, heightened by the water, titillated by Cole's touch. Then, chest to chest, hip to hip, their bodies communicated everything words couldn't.

Cole tasted her skin as he kissed a path from

her breasts to the indentation of her waist. Her hands tangled in his hair, then dug into his shoulders as she clung so close they were nearly one. Urgent, passionate.

"Cole?" It was a plea. She heard it in the tremors he was creating, the quake her body had become.

Her neck was long and slim and vulnerable. He groaned as she arched her back, exposing more of her throat. Dark hair spilled back over her shoulders at the motion.

Her beauty was so much more than the skin he stroked, the eyes that drew him in. It was her spirit, the joy, the generosity of her heart.

Her mouth was greedy as she kissed his jaw, then traveled over his chest. She reached that border at his waist and she felt him suck in his breath. Confidence drew her hands over his thighs until she paused between them.

With a tortured grunt, his arms stretched around her, shifting her. Each subsequent stroke of his hands deepened the heat.

He took her breast in his mouth and she sighed in such pleasure she fisted her hands in his hair. And when his tongue traced a path over her abdomen, her desire fired.

His mouth came back to meet hers. Their legs tangled, he nudged her chin upward, lifting her face so that he could look at her.

Her assent was in her eyes, her mouth, her hands as she arched toward him. His letters had imprinted themselves in her mind, her heart. Now she wanted to imprint him on her body. All of him.

And for now…for all that mattered, they were one.

CHAPTER EIGHTEEN

THE MORNING LIGHT was soft, tempered by the fierce night, the air cleaned by the huge wash of rain. Tess watched Cole as he slept. As she had done since dawn first lifted the shadows.

Even in sleep, he looked troubled. She suspected even the quietest movement would wake him.

Her heart tightened. As certain as she was of his strength, she was equally sure he would conquer this latest setback. But she hated the desperation she'd seen earlier in his eyes.

As much as she was afraid something could happen to him if he stayed in the Reserves, she didn't want to hurt him by withholding her love.

As though she could.

Even now she itched to stroke the lock of dark hair that fell across his forehead.

Why did he have to be so noble? *Because it*

was the right thing to do, he'd said. Did she want him to sacrifice the sense of honor that made him who he was?

The lump in her throat told her the answer.

His eyes opened, focusing on her immediately. She read his relief, followed by contentment. It was the same contentment that curled in her belly.

Their next kiss was slow, thorough, consuming. Somewhere in her mind she'd thought about rising early to make him breakfast. But the thought faded, overridden by a more urgent need.

And, for the moment, she forgot that her heart would break when she had to say goodbye again.

COLE FOUND Tess in her study. When she saw him, she smiled.

How many more times would he get to see that smile? He swallowed, already feeling the loss. "You look busy."

"Not so much. I just called the restaurant. Joseph has everything under control. And everything's okay at the landmark."

Just as Cole smoothed back the strands of

hair that fell over one of her shoulders, the doorbell rang, sending the dogs into a barking
frenzy.

"You expecting anyone?"

She shook her head. "I'll get rid of whoever
it is."

But a few minutes later, she was back in the
study. "Cole?" She gestured behind her. "It's
Rachel and Jim."

Rachel hugged Cole, surprising him, then
took a chair. "Jim says you don't have a plan of
action yet."

Cole stared at her, then at Tess and Jim. "No."

"Well, I do," Rachel stated.

Tess's expression was uneasy. "Rach, this is
Cole's decision."

"Granted. But, Cole, you're close to all the
men concerned, aren't you?" She sighed. "Of
course you are. And right now you're probably
questioning how any one of them could have
done it, including Jim. I'm not obtuse. I know
how this works. Thing is, Cole, I've been watching the situation ever since Tess put David's
money in. Sorry, but that's the truth. It's the reason I wanted to meet someone on the inside." She
paused and her voice softened. "I just didn't

count on meeting Jim. And he changed everything."

At Cole and Tess's shocked expressions, Rachel cleared her throat. "It made the most sense that your first set of designs were lost through the design department. That was your weakest link, even though Jim was sure it hadn't happened. So I evaluated the setup. The designers clearly have the best opportunities to steal them. And one designer just kept sticking out."

Even though Cole wasn't sure what to think of Rachel, he'd rather believe it was one of the designers than his friends. "Garret?"

Rachel shook her head. "Emily Newsom."

"Emily? That sweet, young woman who thanked me for operating such a family-oriented business?"

"No. Emily Newsom whose uncle owns Alton Tool. I'm investigating NuDesign. It's wound up in a bunch of corporate blindfolding, but I'll bet you it's incorporated in her name, ready to be switched over to Alton."

Jim slumped farther down in his chair. "And she's only had twenty-four hours to find out that much."

Cole leaned his head back and stared at the

ceiling. "I knew Alton wanted my company. I didn't know he was this determined…that he was such a player."

Rachel's expression grew even more determined. "So, we become players, too. And raise the stakes so high, Ms. Emily doesn't have a chance."

RACHEL SAT ACROSS from Emily Newsom in one of Houston's most exclusive, most expensive restaurants.

"Thank you for the lunch, Ms. De Villard," Emily said demurely, "but I can't imagine how my work could've caught your attention."

They'd been chatting now for over an hour. Rachel had primed Emily's pump with flattery and subtle persuasion. It was time to move in for the kill. "Oh, Emily, I don't believe a woman like you undervalues her worth."

Emily slowly replaced her iced tea glass on the table. "Excuse me?"

"You have just the commodity to market."

Emily looked intrigued. "And what would that be?"

"You can sell me NuDesign."

"What makes you think I'd be able to do that?"

"You're good," Rachel replied, feeding what she believed by now to be an enormous ego. "And you're smart. You can go to work for your uncle, make respectable money. Or you can sell me the subsidiary, retire tomorrow."

"The subsidiary?"

"NuDesign. Sell it to me now while it's completely in your name."

Emily's wide eyes didn't give away much. "Say, hypothetically, that I understand you. What are you offering?"

"Five million."

She sucked in a breath. "That's a lot of cash."

"Lucky I know how to get my hands on it. Fast."

Emily's gaze appraised her. "I'll call you."

"No." Rachel reached for her purse. "I'll call you."

After a moment's hesitation, the younger woman nodded.

And Rachel knew she'd won.

THE TOWN HOUSE study now resembled a boardroom, littered with half drunk cups of coffee and piles of faxes Rachel was wading through.

The regret in Jim's eyes was real. "I'm sorry, Cole."

"For catching the thief? I'm not."

"No. For hiring Emily in the first place. Hell, I even let her help with the envelope. That must be when she switched the designs. I was so sure I kept the new designs safe. I wouldn't have let anything happen to them if—"

Cole pulled him into a bear hug. "I know that. Thank God Rachel can get us out of this mess. I still don't know how she ever figured out it was Emily in the first place."

"Call it feminine intuition…jealousy," Rachel muttered.

"Jealous?" Jim muttered. "Of that horrible *child?* When I'm dating such a beautiful woman?"

Uncharacteristically, Rachel blushed. "Are we going to get on with this or not?" she demanded. "Lucky I know exactly how to fake a wire transfer. And I have a Justice agent in my debt as well. Men…" she muttered. But she sneaked a look at Jim. And her blush deepened.

THE ATMOSPHERE in the conference room at Harrington's was tense. But Emily was controlled.

Perhaps being twenty-two years old and knowing you're coming into five million dollars did that for a person.

Rachel had drawn up the sale papers with precision, then given them to Brad LaBlanc, Cole's attorney, who was also sitting in on the meeting. In addition, Rachel's justice friend, Donald Slocumbe, along with a notary public and Jim sat quietly around the table.

Emily skimmed over the papers, pausing only when she got to the price: ten dollars and other consideration. "What's this?"

Rachel gave her the completed wire receipt for five million dollars. "That's only legal terminology... I'm sure you're familiar with the way most transfer of ownership documents are phrased for tax purposes."

"Oh." Emily examined the receipt. Then, trying to appear as though she negotiated huge deals every day, she signed.

Cole countersigned each page, making NuDesign a wholly owned subsidiary of Harrington Engineering.

Brad checked each signature, then handed the pages to the notary, who signed and sealed them.

"It's a done deal," Rachel declared.

Tess brought in a tray of champagne and caviar. "Seems a celebration's in order."

Emily looked startled, then accepted a glass of bubbly, downing it quickly.

"I'm glad this worked out well for everyone," Emily said, digging into the caviar, obviously content to forget that the exchange had cost Cole five million dollars.

"You'll be retiring young," Tess agreed, refilling her glass.

Emily laughed. "My uncle would kill me if he knew. I mean he put me through school and everything. Not that I *wanted* to be a software designer, but he's such a control freak, you know?"

"Have some more caviar," Rachel offered. "Tess buys only the best."

"It's very good. My uncle's cheap about stuff like that. Thinks a good meal is barbecue. Thank God I'll have my own money." She downed her second glass of champagne, which Tess refilled.

"But he did get you started on your career."

"Career!" With an embarrassed laugh, she winked at Cole. "The only reason he pushed me to work here is so I could get inside and, well, you know."

"Wasn't that hard? Taking the new designs?"

"Not really." She held up two fingers, indicating a small size between them. "The flash disks are tiny, easy to put in my pocket." She glanced over at Jim. "And, sorry, but you're easy to get by."

Cole couldn't stay still. "And my laptop with the backed-up designs?"

She picked up the wire transfer receipt, then shrugged. "Easy. I wiped them off the hard drive, which might've raised more questions than a missing laptop. But I couldn't very well have walked out the door with the computer, so I put it in a file cabinet going to auction."

He kept his face expressionless, but he had to know. "Why was your uncle so determined to get my designs?"

She took another swallow of her champagne. "He's had it in for you ever since Bosnia."

"Bosnia?" Cole walked around the table. "I didn't know Alton in Bosnia."

"His best friend's kid was in your unit and got killed by friendly fire. My uncle said it was your fault."

Cole stared at Nate who'd been with him during that exchange. They'd both been lucky enough to come back alive.

Rachel cleared her throat. "We're a long way from Bosnia now, Emily. And I have some bad news for you. We've been videotaping this discussion." She pointed to the hidden cameras installed for the party. "And you just admitted to stealing the designs."

Emily's expression sobered. "But we had a deal."

"If you'll read what you signed, the papers say, for ten dollars and other consideration, Harrington Engineering now owns NuDesign."

"You said that was the way legal documents are written and you showed me the wire transfer!" Emily said, her breathing beginning to get shaky. "I have the receipt!"

"Well, about that wire transfer. I'm afraid it's a fake." Rachel handed her a crisp ten dollar bill. "This, however, is entirely genuine."

"I'll sue!" Emily shrieked.

"That might be difficult." Rachel motioned for her friend. "This is Donald Slocumbe of the justice department. Donald, would you show her your identification?"

He pulled out his badge.

"Emily, if you try, Donald will have to preempt you and I doubt you'll enjoy the accommodations at the federal prison. And if your uncle finds out why you signed the papers, I doubt you'll enjoy his either." Rachel took a step forward. "My advice would be to forget about NuDesign."

Emily whirled around. Seeing them all staring at her she threw her glass, but it bounced harmlessly off the Sheetrock wall. Swearing, she rushed from the room.

The rest of them took a collective breath.

"Did it work?" Cole asked.

Rachel thumped a pen on the table. "Yeah."

He kissed her cheek. "Thank you."

She looked pleased. "You're welcome."

Then he turned to Tess. And he saw it in her eyes. The question. Had he been the one responsible for the death of Alton's friend's son?

RUTGER ALTON was a hard man. It showed in his face, his stance, the severe cut of his clothes, the spartan furnishings of his office. His close-cropped steel-gray hair. And his bright blue eyes missed nothing.

It wasn't only that Cole didn't feel welcome. Alton's anger was like heat in the cold room.

"It's about NuDesign." Cole slid a file across the cleared space on the desk.

Alton seemed to hate to take his eyes off Cole long enough to read the papers inside. When he did, he didn't allow much emotion to cross his face. "You expect me to believe these are genuine?"

"One of the witnesses is from the justice department."

Alton closed the folder.

Cole wanted to end the animosity. "Emily says you think I'm responsible for your friend's son's death in Bosnia."

Alton blinked. "You were the officer in charge."

"It was friendly fire."

"Easy excuse for an officer."

Cole couldn't figure out where Alton was coming from. "Were you there?"

"No. But Donny was. Eighteen, joined the Army because he didn't have anything. Not like you, college man. Then you had to come back here and start competing right across town."

"I didn't give that order, not that it matters. I know the sacrifice he made, his family made.

I'm sorry you think I'd take something like that lightly. I'm in the Reserves, Mr. Alton. I joined so they'd pay for my college. I put my education to the best use I knew how by starting my company. I'm not going to apologize for that. We have two options. You tell Mason what happened. Or I show him the new ownership. It's up to you."

COLE KNEW Tess was happy his company had been saved. She'd told him so. Repeatedly. Even now she was taking off from work to hear about Alton. She'd made dinner and was serving it in her courtyard.

Tess passed him the salsa. "He refused to admit his involvement?"

"It doesn't really matter. I meet with Mason in the morning to show transfer of ownership. The designs are ours, the profits are ours. I'd just hoped to work things out with Alton."

She hesitated. "He didn't want to talk?"

Cole met her gaze. "Tess, I wasn't the one who gave the order."

The gentle breeze ruffled the fronds of the banana tree. "I didn't ask."

"But you wanted to know."

"That's all it was then?"

"We were all caught in the blast. Doesn't always happen that way. Sometimes the officers are miles away and don't get touched and enlisted men are the only casualties."

"But you could have been."

"I wasn't."

Even though the light was dim, he could see how pale she was. "But how many times can you come close? Beat the odds?"

"Tess, there aren't any guarantees."

"Exactly! And you know there'll be more deployments, not less. All over the world… Can't you see that? Can't you see you won't be safe?"

"Life isn't always about safety, Tess. What about the future? Don't you want that to be safe, too?"

She bit her bottom lip. "Yes…but—"

"How are we going to make that happen?"

"I don't know…"

"I do. Tess, it's not the other guy's responsibility. It's mine."

"How many people do *I* have to lose?"

He took her hand. "I'm not trying to die. I want to live. With you. Don't push me away, Tess. Don't let this push us apart."

CHAPTER NINETEEN

TESS WAS UNNERVED when her parents invited her over. Worried that something was wrong, she asked for details by phone, but they wouldn't budge. Tess knew no one had been injured or killed because they were meeting over lunch.

All three Spencers away from the restaurants at the same time.

That alone had her anxious.

But the atmosphere in her parents' home was relaxed. Her mother was putting the final touches on a salad when Tess came in the back door, dropping her purse on a stool, then crossing the kitchen to stand beside the older woman.

"Mom?" Tess kissed her cheek. "What is it?"

Judith chuckled. "Patience never was your strong suit. We're eating on the patio." She pointed to the salad. "Would you carry this outside? Your dad has everything else prepared."

Tess took the bowl, trailing her mother, who carried a basket of fragrant baguettes.

"Tessie." Her dad greeted her with a hug.

The table was set with casual dishes, linen napkins and newly cut roses from the bushes that bordered the yard.

That only increased her anxiety. This had to be something big. Otherwise they wouldn't be so utterly calm as though being away from the restaurants was a normal everyday event.

Being raised as part of a restaurant legacy, however, she knew better than to ruin the meal. So she sat in her place and smoothed a napkin over her lap.

"Iced tea all right?" Judith asked.

Tess nodded. At least they didn't think she needed to be anesthetized with anything stronger.

She made it through buttering her bread, adding lemon to her tea.

"Dad—"

"Thomas," Judith prompted her husband.

Tess looked at him expectantly.

He wouldn't be rushed. "Your mother and I have been thinking over a serious decision for some time."

Tess leaned forward, remembering the dreadful moment they'd heard the news about David. Her breath shortened.

"You're not ill, are you, Dad?"

He patted her hand. "No. It's nothing like that. But we did want to talk to you away from the restaurant."

She blinked. That was something new.

He took Judith's hand. "Tess, we're ready to spend more time with each other rather than the restaurant."

Even though they'd shown signs of stress, it was a difficult concept to take in. "You mean retire?"

Her parents exchanged glances. "We'd like to keep a hand in it, but not on a daily basis."

Tess slumped back in her chair.

"You okay, sweetie?" her mother asked.

"Yes, sure." Tess shook her head. "I'm just surprised."

"We know." Judith glanced at her husband. "It wasn't an easy decision."

Thomas sighed. "Losing David made us realize we didn't have forever to do the things we've always said we would."

Tess swallowed a rush of emotion, unable to speak.

"Things have changed." Judith's voice wobbled. "And we can't turn back the days…. It's time we learned how to deal with our life as it is now…to deal with change itself."

Tess made herself stay strong for her parents. In truth, she wanted nothing more than to break down in the safety of their arms and sob.

"Spencers is important to us." Thomas met her eyes. "But we don't want you to become a slave to the business. You've worked too hard since David died. The hours…the commitment… We're grateful to you, Tessie. We couldn't have gone on without you. But we want more for you, too."

Tess tried but failed to stop her tears.

"So, if you're agreeable," he continued, "we'd like you to take over the landmark, with plenty of help. And we're hoping we can recruit from the family again. Find another De Villard who will make sure you don't spend every waking hour working."

"When you have your own family, you'll want someone who can share running the landmark," Judith added. "Your father and I were lucky. We had each other."

Her father leaned forward. "You were right

about bringing in the boys. I think Joseph can take over for you at the Galleria. And Eric is doing well in Galveston."

Stunned by his acceptance, Tess stared at her father. She'd seen the aging, the fatigue. But she had believed it was something they could get past. Until now.

The torch was being passed. In the quiet of the home she had grown up in with her twin.

Tess clasped a hand of each of her parents. She had thought that, somehow, by keeping them all in place at the restaurants, she could prevent another major shift in their lives.

A breeze ruffled the leaves of the weeping willow.

Her chest tightened. Everything was changing again…and it was beyond her control.

BY NIGHTFALL, Tess rattled around her office. Joseph was competently handling the dinner crowd, as he'd done in the past weeks. She saw on a daily basis that he loved what he was doing. It was the family connection.

Which left the landmark.

Always run by the head of the Spencer family. She'd never imagined a time her father wouldn't be involved. But if pressed, she could've seen David taking that inevitable step.

Feeling so alone she wanted to cry, Tess had to get out of there. To find the one person she could lean on.

She grabbed her purse, then dashed outside through the back. She headed out the garage, cell phone in hand. But Cole wasn't in his office.

Hoping he'd be at home, she drove faster than usual, speeding past slower vehicles, dodging squalls in the traffic. Turning down his street, she caught her breath. There was a light on in his house.

When he opened the door, she all but fell into his arms.

"Tess? What's wrong?"

She couldn't speak, her face buried in his shirt.

"It's not one of your parents, is it?"

She shook her head.

"One of the cousins?"

"No," she muttered.

He patted her back. "No one's hurt or sick?"

She burrowed deeper against his chest. "No."

As if he knew exactly what she needed, he

simply stood and held her. His touch was gentle but strong. And he pressed a soft kiss on top of her head.

Finally she felt calm enough to step back. "You must think I've gone around the bend." She pushed at her hair.

He watched her carefully. But he didn't voice the questions in his eyes.

Grateful, she leaned against him as he guided her to the sofa. They sat still for a long time.

"Do you want to tell me about it?"

Nodding, she started to speak and the words took over, spilling out of her. "I can still barely take it in," she finished.

"Isn't this good in the long run?"

"It's…"

"Everything's changing again," he said.

"I'm terrified that if…" her voice choked "…they retire…they might die before their time."

"If retirement doesn't make them happy, they can always come back to work." He stroked her hair. "Maybe this is what they need to survive. They've spent a lot of years preserving the family legacy. Maybe they need to build something new, just for themselves."

It had never occurred to her. "Maybe," she replied cautiously.

He tucked one errant strand of hair over her shoulder. "It's something most of us need."

COLE DIDN'T PRESS, spending hours keeping her calm. And when she finally fell into an exhausted sleep, he kept watch. Restless and disturbed, her sleep was fitful.

By dawn, she'd fallen into a deeper sleep, so he eased out of bed. Making sure to be quiet, he found Tess's keys in her purse. Then he left the house, taking advantage of the empty streets to drive to Tess's town house and collect her pets. He'd called to make sure the busboy went by to feed and walk them the previous evening, but Tess had worried about leaving them untended. And right now, she didn't need anything else to worry about.

Hector and Molly greeted him excitedly, following him to Tess's bedroom, where he found a change of casual clothing. Then he got the animals' crates, leashes and food. He packed it all, along with them, into his car. When he arrived back home, he put the dogs in the backyard and took Scat inside. Tess was still asleep.

His own cats leaped up on the bookcases, cautiously watching the stranger.

Cole brewed a pot of coffee, glad he'd put in a supply of food. He'd done it because of Tess. He wandered over to the sleek gallery doors that led to the backyard. He'd made a lot of changes in his life because of her.

Could he make another?

She wouldn't commit to him if he stayed in the Reserves. Her fear was real, so he'd searched his conscience. For all that was pushing him to serve, he knew her fear wasn't misplaced. There was danger in every deployment. And he couldn't promise he'd return from one or all of them. But could he give up what meant so much to him?

Hearing her stir, he walked back into the bedroom. Scat had jumped up on the bed and was kneading her shoulders. Still groggy, she stroked the cat's fur. Then she opened her eyes. And jerked upright.

"I brought Scat," Cole explained. "Molly and Hector are out back."

"What time is it?" Tess asked as she relaxed, hugging Scat.

"Early." Her face was tired, strained, and he

wanted to ease her worry, or least try to. "Which is good since this is a full-out kidnapping."

She looked off balance, then intrigued. "Oh?"

"I already corralled the pets." He pointed to her fresh clothes on a chair. "You're next."

Her first instinct was to refuse. He read that in her face, too, along with the struggle that followed.

"What did you have in mind?" she asked finally.

"Galveston. You, me and the menagerie."

Her eyes widened. "You're willing to take the animals?"

"They're part of the package. And I happen to like the package."

"But what about your work?"

"It can survive without me."

"You don't have to do this."

"Yes. I do." More than he could tell her. More than she would understand.

The colors in her eyes shifted, the stormy gray easing into blue. "You're a surprising man, Cole Harrington."

FEW TOURISTS remained in Galveston after the sunshine gave way to the cooler days of autumn. But the town didn't close down. The *B.O.I.*, born on the island, breathed a collective sigh of relief, able again to reclaim their city.

Tess had always loved Galveston, from the beaches to the Victorian homes, to the remaining glimpses of the town's nineteenth-century glory.

They strolled down the boardwalk, the dogs on their leashes. They'd left the cats behind once Cole had explained his weren't used to cars and would consider it one long, tortuous ride to the vet's.

Tess drew in the clean ocean air. Along with the sound of waves that washed ashore, it had a calming effect.

Seagulls landed on the mostly empty beach, making tracks the water soon erased.

"If someone had asked me what I'd be doing today, I'd never have guessed this," she admitted.

"As opposed to tense strategy meetings?"

"I suppose so." The wind tugged at her hair and she shook it back.

"It took your parents time to make the decision. Give yourself time to accept it."

He was wise. Not just smart. There was a

vast difference. "I never used to think about time. It was just there, not something to be measured."

He tightened his grip on her hand. "You don't have to find the answers today, Tess. That's why I brought you here."

"I don't understand."

"The tide has been going in and out since time began. But has it changed?"

"I suppose not."

"Yet you're expecting yourself to accept radical changes quickly. Think you're stronger than the ocean?"

THE PARTY at the landmark was huge, one that had taken all of Tess's time to organize. Time that kept her away from Cole. It was a celebration to announce the changes at Spencers, to honor Judith and Thomas.

Cheers met the announcements, from employees and family. After the speeches, the swing band took over. It was a successful party, one of the best she'd ever managed.

Tess toasted her three favorite cousins. "To the best family ever." Their glasses clinked together.

The vintage champagne suited the emotional moment.

Tess glanced at each of them in turn. "You all mean so much to me."

"Ditto," Sandy chimed in.

"Good grief, you're not going to cry, are you?" Rachel moaned as she patted Tess's back. "Aw, Tessie. It's going to be okay."

Tess held on tight. Rachel, being Rachel, had gone straight to the core of Tess's mixed emotions.

"Your parents look so happy," Kate told her.

Tess followed her gaze. "They do."

Sandy frowned. "You don't sound pleased."

"I am. I just…"

"Change," Kate sympathized.

Tess swallowed. "Yes."

"It's been a heck of a year," Sandy commiserated. "Last October, we were rejoicing the end of bathing suit season. And look at us now."

"We seemed more innocent," Kate mused.

You're expecting yourself to accept radical changes quickly. Think you're stronger than the ocean?

As she met her cousins' concerned faces, Tess managed a shaky smile. "I'm like an old log in the forest, all settled in until someone turns me over and exposes my vulnerable side."

Rachel cocked her head. "No. You're a person who's lost a lot, taken on even more. It's okay to be scared. Just remember it's okay to lean, too. Give Cole a chance, Tess." Rachel's expression softened as she watched Cole and Jim approach.

"Dance?" Cole asked Tess.

Their continued intimacy was constant, slow torture. She slipped her hand in his, aware of the approving looks from her cousins.

The music was soft, a sweet song of love and promise. As Cole guided her around the dance floor, she tried to imagine her life without him. The pain intensified.

He seemed to know, pulling her closer. She wanted to rail at the irony. She *didn't* want to change him. Just his one inexorable decision.

"I've missed you," he murmured against her hair.

Tess closed her eyes. Despite the flurry that her life had been since her father's decision, a minute hadn't gone by without missing him.

The song's evocative notes seemed to underscore her ebbing resistance. Yet Tess didn't think she could survive accepting him, then losing him. She no longer believed that was a remote possibility. Media casualty counts weren't real unless you loved one of those casualties.

As the last strains of the song faded, it was replaced by an upbeat swing number. Tess was relieved that Cole didn't expect her to dance to the fast, cheerful tune. They wound their way to the edge of the dance floor. And nearly ran straight into her father.

Thomas caught her by the hand. "Do you mind if I steal my little girl for a few minutes, Cole?"

"No, sir."

But Tess felt his eyes on her as she and her dad walked away from the crowd.

"You've done a good job," Thomas told her.

"I've got a lot of experience," she murmured, trying to keep sight of Cole.

"No."

She snapped back to face him. "What?"

"I'm saying you've done a good job accepting all these changes, honey. I know it's not what you want, but you've stepped up to the plate like you always do."

Her mouth trembled.

"What is it, Tess?"

She bit her bottom lip, trying to stave off the tears. "You're wrong, Dad. I'm not stepping up, I can't even get to the ballpark."

"You mean Cole."

She nodded.

"What's the problem?"

"I'm a coward."

"I don't believe that."

"Believe it, Dad. Cole intends to stay in the Reserves. And I can't handle that. If I lost someone else…"

Thomas squeezed her hand. "You know that your grand-uncles didn't survive World War II. But I don't think I ever told you about my father's guilt over that."

"Grandpa?"

"He couldn't understand why he was spared when they weren't. It was with him every day of his life. Yet he was the one who *did* come home. Just like the pain of losing your brother will be in my heart until I take my last breath. But losing is part of living. What would I do differently? Not have the children I love so much?" He chucked one hand under her chin. "Or raise

David not to honor his heritage? No. But I do want him remembered with purpose and pride. Which, in a sense, is all Cole is asking. To be allowed to do what he believes in."

"What if he's killed, too?"

"Tess, we're all scared of one thing or another. But if you think your life would be empty if you married Cole and then lost him, think how empty it will be if you walk away."

"I know, but—" Her voice choked.

"You love him, Tess. And he loves you."

"He hasn't said that, Dad."

"He says it in every look and gesture when you're together. Tess, don't mourn something that hasn't happened yet."

She'd trusted her father all her life.

"Go," he said softly. "Don't waste one second of this glorious life."

She hugged him fiercely, then went to find Cole.

He was on the terrace. He stood at the railing looking out at the surrounding skyscrapers. Far below, the traffic was muted.

As she watched, he turned.

Her steps were surprisingly sure as she crossed the distance between them.

"Tess?"

She searched his familiar face. How had she ever believed she could walk away from him? "The party's winding down."

"Everything all right with your dad?"

She grasped her newfound courage. "Very all right." Despite the low lights, she glimpsed concern in the brilliant blue of his eyes. But there was something else in them, something she hadn't seen before. Despair.

Knowing she'd put it there, hating herself for it, she stroked his face. "There's something I've never told you."

"Oh?"

"I've never told you how much I think David would've liked you."

He stood still; swallowed hard. "That means a lot to me."

Tess stepped closer. "You mean a lot to me."

"Oh, Tess." His voice was raw, husky.

Her courage seemed to be flowing unstopped now. "I love you, Cole."

For a moment it seemed he hadn't heard her. But then he smiled.

"And," she continued, clutching her courage close, "I don't want to change you. I love you because you're honorable and noble and…I can accept that means you have to serve."

He lowered his mouth to kiss her. "I love you too much to let you live in fear, Tess."

Her breathing stalled, as she realized she might have already lost him.

"I've given for my country. Now I want to give to you. I've thought a lot about it… I can keep serving by helping vets like Ron. But if you'll marry me, I'm done with the Reserves."

She trembled with a sense of exploding hope. "You have to be sure, Cole."

"Is that a yes?"

Glorious life, her father had said. "Oh, very much. Yes, yes!"

He lifted her, spinning her around the secluded space next to the city's giant buildings. Until their mouths met again in a kiss of promise and happiness.

And this time, when her world tilted, it was more glorious than she could ever have dreamed.

EPILOGUE

TESS PEEKED around the towering, stone arch. She could see the guests taking their seats in the pews of the hundred-year-old church. Tall pewter candelabras held dozens of candles. Exquisite calla lilies decorated the chapel. The beautiful autumn day delivered bright sunshine that lit the stained glass windows and reached the lofty beams.

Judith fussed so emphatically with the train on Tess's gown that she angled her head, trying to see.

Her mother rose from a kneeling position, her lips suddenly trembling as she faced Tess.

"Mom?"

Tears glinted in Judith's eyes. "You're so beautiful."

Not caring about makeup or hair, Tess hugged her tightly.

Judith hung on for several moments, reluctantly releasing her. "I don't want to crush your gorgeous dress."

It was a gown they'd chosen together. The formfitting bodice ended in a graceful full, pearl-beaded skirt with a long train. It was exquisitely elegant. Like this day, it was matchless.

Judith gently touched Tess's face. "Keep this joy in your heart, and always know how proud we are, how much we love you."

"You're going to make me cry!"

"None of that." Judith smiled. And although her tone was brisk, her eyes were misty. "Now, I'd better let that handsome young brother of Cole's escort me to my seat."

"I love you, Mom."

Judith kissed her cheek.

Before Tess could cry, her three musketeers stepped in. She'd chosen them all as her maids of honor. After all, it was *her* wedding. And, she couldn't choose one over the other two.

They wore champagne colored gowns, but the resemblance ended there. The cut of each was chosen to complement the woman. Kate's was soft, romantic. Sandy's, surprisingly sexy. Rachel's simple but dramatic.

Rachel adjusted a fold in Tess's dress.

"There's a pretty handsome guy at the other end of the church who's waiting for you."

"Do tell?"

Rachel's expression softened. "You look perfect."

Sandy aligned a tendril of hair that escaped Tess's elegant upsweep. "I always knew you'd be first."

"You never told me that."

Kate fiddled with the veil. "It's because you're so romantic."

"Me?"

"I know you think it's me." Kate smiled wisely. "But you're the true romantic."

Tess pleaded silently with Rachel for help.

"Just enjoy. Besides, your father's going to wear a hole in the floor. And, yes, I know it's a stone floor."

Tess laughed. "You three…"

"Ready?" Rachel asked.

"Yes."

At Rachel's signal, Tess's aunt Susan started the flower girls, two young cousins, and the ring bearer, another. The guests, many related to the children, oohed and aahed as the girls dropped white rose petals on the carpeted aisle.

When the children stood at the altar, the first maid of honor emerged. Walking up the aisle in order of their birth, appropriate since Tess was the youngest, Sandy went first. She kissed Tess's cheek, winked, then walked sedately through the arch carrying a bouquet of white roses.

Kate was next. Beaming, she squeezed Tess's hand. "I wish you happiness forever."

Rachel waited for the others to take their timed steps forward before turning to Tess. "You are well loved." Then she, too, was gone.

Tess bent to sniff the bouquet Cole had picked for her. Lush with calla lilies and orchids it was as remarkable as the man himself.

Thomas took his place beside her.

Tess clutched his arm for strength. "Oh, Dad."

"Happy, Tessie?"

"Very."

He patted her arm. "You look incredibly beautiful. Almost as beautiful as the day you were born. Are you ready?"

She nodded.

He kissed her cheek. Taking a deep breath, they started the age-old tradition. One that felt so right.

Tess hung on to him as they eased beneath the high arch, suddenly in sight of all the guests.

Every pew was packed. Even though the rafters soared more than two stories above the church seemed awfully full.

She spotted Ron and Mary, as well as Cole's friends from his plant and the Reserves. As they walked closer to the front, she saw his parents and siblings, relatives on all sides who'd flown in for the wedding.

Her gaze skipped across Allen, the best man.

She wanted to see *her* man.

Cole was magnificent in a gray and black morning suit. So elegant, so handsome. Tucked in the lapel was a miniature calla lily that matched her bouquet.

His eyes were shining, full of love. Her throat swelled with all she felt for him.

The familiar words washed over her as she stood beside him, as he took her hand in his and exchanged vows she took for eternity.

Reverend Harper smiled as he said the words, "I now pronounce you husband and wife. You may kiss the bride."

Cole was tender and joyous as he lifted her veil. "For keeps," he whispered.

As they kissed, she sealed the words to her heart.

"May I present Mr. And Mrs. Cole Harrington," Reverend Harper announced.

Everyone stood. Smiles were as abundant as the air, but Tess and Cole smiled the most. At each other. Their families, friends.

But mostly at each other.

When Tess and Cole arrived at the landmark Spencers for the reception, everyone broke into applause.

Spencers had hosted its share of celebrities, diplomats and presidents, but nobody as important as Tess and Cole.

A small orchestra provided the music.

Cole offered his arm to his bride. "Dance, Mrs. Harrington?"

She tucked up her train. "Delighted, Mr. Harrington."

The waltz might have come from another century, but the emotion between them was strictly in the present.

"It's real," she murmured as they spun around the fairy-tale room.

His fingers curled around hers. "Does that mean I can blink?"

"You feel it, too?"

His eyes held hers. "That you're part of me forever?"

Her lips trembled. "And ever."

"Then it's real."

HARLEQUIN *Super*ROMANCE®

**A powerful new story from a
RITA® Award-nominated author!**

A Year and a Day
by **Inglath Cooper**

**Harlequin Superromance #1310
On sale November 2005**

Audrey Colby's life is the envy of most. She's
married to a handsome, successful man, she
has a sweet little boy and they live in a lovely
home in an affluent neighborhood. But
everything is not always as it seems. Only
Nicholas Wakefiled has seen the danger
Audrey's in. Instead of helping, though,
he complicates things even more....

Available wherever Harlequin books are sold.

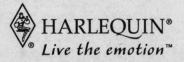

HARLEQUIN®
Live the emotion™